ALSO BY ELIZABETH BERG

Ordinary Life

RANDOM HOUSE • NEW YORK

Elizabeth Berg

Ordinary Life

STORIES

RANDOM HOUSE and colophon are registered trademarks
of Random House, Inc.

Some of the stories in this work have been previously published
in *Family Circle, Good Housekeeping, New Woman, Special Report,* and *Woman.*

Library of Congress Cataloging-in-Publication Data
Berg, Elizabeth.
Ordinary life : stories / Elizabeth Berg.
p.   cm.
ISBN 0-679-43746-0
1. United States—Social life and customs—20th century—Fiction.
2. Women—United States—Fiction.   3. Domestic fiction, American.
4. Love stories, American.   I. Title.
PS3552.E6996 O74 2002
813'.54—dc21   2001041754

Printed in the United States of America on acid-free paper
Random House website address: www.atrandom.com

24689753

FIRST EDITION

Book design by Carole Lowenstein

For Kate Medina
with great love and respect

Contents

Ordinary Life

Ordinary Life:
A Love Story

Mavis McPherson is locked in the bathroom and will not come out. The tub is lined with pillows and blankets. Under the sink, next to the extra toilet paper, there is an economy-sized box of Wheat Thins, a bowl of apples, and a six-pack of Heath bars. Against the wall, under the towel rack, is a case of Orangina, and next to that is a neat pile of magazines and three library books. A spiral-bound notebook and pen lie on top of the toilet tank. Hanging from the hook on the back of the door are several changes of underwear.

Mavis is on retreat, she tells her husband through the crack in the door when he comes home that evening. Al volunteers at St. Mary's Hospital, dividing his time between delivering newspapers to patients and helping maintenance fix faulty equipment, though this is a secret from the administration—volunteers aren't supposed to do that. Al's mechanical skills are legendary, but he is not known for his sense of humor. "Come on, Mavis," he sighs. "What's for dinner?"

"You might as well go on over to Big Boy," Mavis tells him. "I'm not cooking dinner. I'm not coming out for a week or so. It's nothing personal." She leans her ear against the crack in the door, listening for his response.

She hears only the wheezy sounds of him breathing in and out. She's afraid Al has emphysema, but he won't go to a doctor. "See 'em enough at the hospital," he always says. "Stuffy little bastards." She tries to look through the crack in the door, sees a tiny slice of Al's blue shirt, a piece of his ear. "Let me in, Mavis," he finally says, rattling the doorknob. "I gotta use the can."

"You know perfectly well we have another bathroom. You'll have to use that."

"I don't like that one. And it doesn't have a bathtub."

"Well, I know that."

"So how am I supposed to shower?" Al likes to shower in the evening, a characteristic Mavis has never liked, finding it somehow effeminate. Overall, though, she has few complaints. She loves Al dearly.

"You'll have to ask the neighbors," Mavis says. "Or maybe the Y. I'll bet the Y would let you shower there."

Silence. Then Al says, "What is this, Mavis, a fight? Is it a fight?"

She steps back, fingers the ruffled collar of her white blouse. "Why, *no,*" she says, a little surprised. "I just got an idea that I really want some time completely to myself. And I'm taking it. I don't see the point in running off somewhere. We can't afford it anyway. Can we?"

Nothing.

"So," she says, "I'll stay right here. I don't need anything but some quiet. I want to be in a small room, alone, to just . . . relax, and not do anything else. I was thinking of the ocean, but this is fine."

"Oh, boy. I'm calling the kids," Al says. "And I'm calling Dr. Edelson or Edelman or whoever that robber is that you go to every twenty minutes. You've gone around the bend this time, Mavis. What have you got in there, Alzheimer's? Is that it?" He knocks loudly at the door. "Mavis, have you lost your goddamn mind?"

Mavis goes to the mirror to look at herself, tightens one of her pearl studs that has loosened, then walks back to the door. "I am seventy-nine years old, Al," she says softly, into the crack.

"What's that?"

"I say I'm seventy-nine years old," she says, louder.

He inhales sharply. "Aw, jeez. This is about my missing your *birth*day?"

"It's not my birthday for five months, Al. Remember? I was born in December. In a blizzard. Remember?"

"Well, I'm calling the kids," Al says. "Yes sir. All three of them. Right now." She hears his voice moving down the hall. "And your doctor, too."

"That's not necessary," Mavis calls out. And then, yelling, "Al? I'm not going crazy. I'm just thinking. I was going to tell you about this, but you . . ."

He can't hear her. She sits down on the closed seat of the toilet, peels the wrapper off a candy bar. "I am seventy-nine years old," she says aloud, and takes a bite. This is the beginning of what she wanted to say. Truthfully, she wasn't sure what would come next; she figured it would just happen, naturally. She examines the candy bar as she chews. She has always liked this, looking at food while she eats it. Makes it taste better. She wonders how they get that curly little swirl on the top of every candy bar. It's a nice touch, even though some machine did it and it is therefore not sincere. She crosses her legs, gently swings the top one, then leans over to the side to inspect it. She used to have great legs. "Oh, honey," Al had said the first time he undid her garters and pulled her nylons off. "Look at these gams." He had kissed her thighs, and she blushed so furiously she thought surely he'd see it in the dark. They were on their honeymoon, in a cottage in the Adirondacks. Her hair had been long and honey blonde, pulled back at the sides by two tortoiseshell combs, curled under at the bottom in a pageboy. The Andrews Sisters were on the radio at the moment she lost her virginity, her white negligee raised high over her breasts, one comb fallen off and digging into her shoulder, though not unpleasantly. She shook so hard when Al entered her he wanted to stop, but she wouldn't let him. "It's fine, honey," she said. "It just hurts." Her fingers were balled into fists against his back and she uncurled them, tried to relax. She looked for a place on the ceiling to focus on. She'd concentrate on that, take her mind off things.

"I can wait," Al had said. "Why don't I wait?" He'd raised himself up, tried to look into her face. But she hid herself in his shoulder, embarrassed and silent, then giggling.

"I don't think that helps, waiting," she'd finally said. "You just go on ahead. It's all right."

Afterward, they'd made a nest of the blankets and pillows, faced each other in the dim light, spoke in low tones of all the things they wanted to do: candlelit dinners every Saturday night, four children, the biggest Christmas tree on the lot every year. They touched each other's faces with the tips of their fingers, probed gently at the openings between each other's lips. At breakfast the next morning, Al had said Mavis looked different. More womanly. She said she'd noticed exactly the same thing. He took her hand, she put down her fork, and they went back to the bedroom. Already they had a special language, Mavis had thought, and the intimacy grounded her, fueled her. It hadn't hurt so much the second time.

"Hey, Mavis," Al says now, banging on the door. "Jonathan wants to talk to you. He's on the phone. You'd better come out here."

Mavis walks to the door, straightens her skirt, speaks loudly into the crack. "Listen to me, Al. I just told you I want to have a week to myself. I'm not coming out to talk on the telephone to Jonathan or any of the other children. I wish you'd stop running off and just let me *tell* you about this. No need to take offense or to think I'm crazy. For heaven's sake."

"Jonathan is on the phone, long distance," Al says.

Mavis rolls her eyes. "Well, I guess I know it's long distance, Al. If he lives in California and we live in Minnesota, then obviously it's long distance."

"So what am I supposed to say? That his mother can't be bothered talking to him?"

Mavis sighs, thinks for a moment. Jonathan in the Bathinette, his baby fists waving, his palm-sized chest rising up and down excitedly. "Water," Mavis is saying. "Yes, it's *water*, darling." A kerchief is around her head. She is wearing red lipstick and open-toed shoes.

Quietly, Mavis says, "Go and tell Jonathan that I'm fine, Al, that I'll call him in a week. And don't you say anything else. I can hear you, you know!"

She can't, of course, the phone is too far away, but Al doesn't know that. His hearing is starting to go, hers has thus far remained the same, so as far as Al is concerned, Mavis's hearing is suddenly extraordinarily acute.

"And come back after that," Mavis says. "I want to talk to you."

"The hell I will," Al says. "I'm going out."

"Where to?"

"The straitjacket store, that's where."

Big Boy, Mavis thinks. Well, good. When he comes back he'll be in a better mood. He'll get beef because she's not around to tell him not to, probably a cream pie for dessert, too. Fine. Then she'll be able to talk to him. Maybe he'll feel a little guilty about what he ate. That will work entirely to her benefit as well.

She slips off her shoes, climbs into the bathtub, lies back against the pillows. It's really not bad. For once in her life, she is happy she's so short. She wiggles her toes inside her nylons. She should have dressed more casually. She undoes the button on her skirt, then unzips it slightly. There is a tan-colored stain on her blouse between the second and third button. Coffee? She wets her finger, rubs at it. Well, she'll soak it later. It's convenient being in here. She closes her eyes. She's really very comfortable, could probably take a nap right now. But then it will be hard to sleep later on tonight.

She arranges the pillows to act as a backrest and climbs out of the tub to get a magazine. She feels the mean pull of arthritis in her knees. She selects a *Good Housekeeping*, climbs back in the tub, starts flipping through the pages, and realizes she's already looked at this one—there's the place where she tore out the recipe for low-fat lemon chicken.

Mavis used to give all her old magazines to her sister, Eileen, but her sister died last year. Breast cancer. She closes her eyes, lets herself hurt for a moment. The pain has not yet dulled, nor does she expect it to or even want it to.

Mavis and Eileen slept in the same bed as children; until she was eight, Mavis's preamble to sleep was to wrap Eileen's long hair around her fingers, then suck her thumb dreamily while drifting off. She had to make sure Eileen was sleeping first; Eileen got mad if she caught Mavis messing with her hair. Mavis had once tried wrapping her fingers in the folds of a satin doll dress her mother had given her for her birthday, but it wouldn't do—she needed the weighty, coarse silkiness of Eileen's hair. She liked the heat from Eileen's scalp at one end, reminding her of the thrilling fact of life; and the cool and bristly bluntness at the other end was wonderful to twitch your fingers over rapidly. It was worth getting caught every now and then for all that pleasure. The worst that ever happened was the night Mavis didn't wait long enough, and Eileen reared up like a ghost in her white nightgown and socked Mavis three times in the stomach. Otherwise any attack was a sleepy and halfhearted thing that barely hurt, a dull nudge in the rib, a smack on her leg that was off the mark and carried no more weight than a falling towel. And of course, she usually didn't get caught at all.

Mavis had gotten married first, and when Eileen asked her for certain essential details, Mavis had said, "Now, you might want to cry out. But don't." Oh, she missed her. Missed her. The conversations at the kitchen table, their elbows on the embroidered tablecloth, the steam from their coffee cups rising up. They would talk far into the night when they got together every week for dinner, and Al and Big Jim would get so impatient. They were all right as long as the fights were on, or some other sports event, but then the minute that was over, they wanted to go, one or the other of them, back home. When they were at Eileen's house, Al would come to stand at Mavis's shoulder, and she ignored him as long as she was able to. When they were at Mavis's, Big Jim would eventually sit down heavily at the table with them, simultaneously irritated and interested in what could possibly keep them here for so long, what could be so important that they hadn't even taken their aprons off from doing dishes before they sat down. They had just talked yesterday, hadn't they? Hell, they talked every day, didn't they?

On one memorable occasion, Al and Big Jim had both gone to sleep in the living room, both of them on the sofa with their heads back and their mouths open, and the women finally had the chance to completely exhaust themselves. They woke their husbands up at 2 A.M. after they'd taken a picture.

It was a week ago, when Mavis was cleaning out the bedroom closet, that she came across that photo again. It had fallen out of the album, its corner holders still in place but the glue on back dried to a fine dust. Mavis sat down on the bed with the photo, smiling at it. It had zigzag edges, looked to have been cut out with pinking shears. There was a bright spot off to one side of the photo, evidence of the imperfect flash of that time. The men's heads were inclined fraternally toward each other, their mouths open in ways so identical it almost seemed the whole scene was staged. But if you looked a little closer you could tell it wasn't; something about the defenseless posturing of the rest of their bodies, the heartbreaking vulnerability of real sleep: the open hand, the foot off at an odd angle, the sock drooping below the pants leg. The men's faces were so young and unlined Mavis nearly gasped, looking at them. Their shirts were short-sleeved, boxy looking, tucked into the pleated pants the men wore with thin belts. Mavis remembered ironing the shirt Al was wearing, standing in the kitchen with the radio on, potatoes boiling gently on top of the stove. She'd sprinkle the ironing first, using a soda bottle with a special top, then store it in a plastic bag in the refrigerator until she was ready. She used to iron everything, even Al's underwear. She can't remember exactly when she stopped.

Even more than the men in the photo, Mavis found she was interested in the surroundings: There was the sofa they used to have, the nubby floral one, so comfortable—what had happened to that? There, on a table they used to have in the corner, the porcelain figure that had belonged to her mother, that Mavis had later dropped and broken when she was dusting, then sat and wept over when neither she nor Al could repair it. She hadn't really liked it, but it was her mother's. And her mother was gone.

Mavis had sighed, put down her dust rag. She had lain back on the bed and closed her eyes, the photo facedown on her stomach, her hand over it. She'd wished she had more pictures of everything she used to have—all her furniture, even her old refrigerator, and what was in it, too: the big, square blocks of butter in the ribbed glass container, the old flowered mixing bowls she used to have holding leftovers, covered with waxed paper and anchored with rubber bands. How could she have known that ordinary life would have such allure later on?

What plants used to be in their house? she wondered. What stamps were on the envelopes that came in the mail? How exactly did the wringer washer look, the newspaper, the bathroom scale she used to weigh herself on? Their bedroom wallpaper, didn't it use to be flowered, those big cabbage roses? Where was the pink girdle she used to have? It had a matching brassiere with wide satin straps.

Mavis had opened her eyes and looked out the bedroom window, sighing, watching the breeze lift the leaves on the trees outside. It came to her that she wasn't quite sure where in her life she was. Near the end, she supposed. Certainly more near the end than the beginning. Most of what a life is for, she had done: Her children were grown and had children of their own; she was retired from the job she'd taken after the youngest left home. She had traveled with Al to the extent that they were able; she had taken adult education courses, contributed as generously as she could to causes she believed in. What now? Really, *what*, now?

"Enough!" she'd said then, out loud, and she'd gotten up to go back to the closet and look for the album where the photo belonged. She found the album, even the right place for the photo. On the black page, in white ink, she had written in a careful, dainty script, "The boys, mesmerized. June 8, 1946." Well, no more "girls" looking at the "boys," asleep or awake. No more girls.

Big Jim had dropped by frequently right after Eileen died, sat stunned-looking at the kitchen table, his hands folded, watching Mavis make dinner and then eating with them. But lately he hadn't come around. Able, finally, to stay home, Mavis decided. Or visiting others, perhaps. She and Eileen were so close it preempted other friendships, they both admitted that. Maybe now that Eileen was dead, Big Jim had made new friends. She hoped so. She knew her resemblance to Eileen was hard for Jim to bear. Hard for her, too.

Mavis starts awake, knocking her head slightly against the side of the tub. Outside the door, Al is calling her name. "One minute," she calls, and the absurd thought comes to her that she should put on a robe. Then she shakes her head, clearing it, and goes to the door. "Hi, honey," she says, into the crack. "How are you? Did you eat?"

"Mavis, you get the hell out of that bathroom, right now."

"Al—"

"I'm not going to listen to any of your bull crap about a retreat,

Mavis. Now, so far I haven't done anything about it. But this is your last chance before I do."

"Yes, you did do something about it. You called Jonathan."

"I *pretended* to call Jonathan."

"Well!" she says. And then, because she cannot help it, she says again, "Well!"

"You come out of there right now. Or I will . . . do something."

She waits, and then he says, "What the hell would you do if *I* did this, Mavis? What would you think?"

"I would help you, Al," she says.

"What? Speak up, I can't hear you."

"I say, I would *help* you!" She means to be tender, but it is difficult when you're yelling.

Behind the door, Al grunts.

"I would try to understand," she says. "I wouldn't think it was so crazy, needing to get away from the world for a while. I would just let you do it, and I would talk to you when you wanted to talk, and when you needed things I would bring them to you, and I would not try to make you feel bad and guilty."

Silence. And in it, his recognition that she is absolutely right.

She hears him shuffling about, changing his position, and then there is the long and heavy sound of him sliding down against the door and onto the floor. And then nothing. Is he all right? Oh, this is a terrible trick. Shame on him.

If it's a trick.

She knocks rapidly at the door. "Al? *Al?*"

"What."

"Are you all right?"

"Yeah!"

"Well—what are you doing?"

"I don't know, Mavis. Did you say you wanted to talk to me?"

She sits down on the floor, too, opposite him, as far as she can tell. "You know, honey," she says, "I'm kind of tired now. I think I'd like to go to sleep."

"How can you sleep in there, Mavis?"

"Oh, it's fine. I lined the tub with all kinds of blankets. It's cozy!"

"Do you have a nightgown?"

Oh, God. What else has she forgotten? "I don't need one."

She hears him walk away down the hall, and then he is back again, knocking. "Mavis? I've got your pink one, here. Is that all right?"

She smiles, opens the door, and takes the nightgown. His face is so full of something, she kisses him quickly, even if it's cheating. Then she closes the door softly, says through it, " 'Night, honey."

"Good night."

"Take your pills."

"I know. Mavis?"

"Yes?"

"We've never spent a night apart."

"I know."

She turns out the light, feels her way back to the bathtub, and climbs in. This day passed so quickly. And has really been so interesting. Perhaps she should have said she'd be in here longer than a week.

"Mavis?"

She opens her eyes. A thin light. Early morning. She stretches, turns toward the door, speaks loudly. "Yes?"

"Are you coming out today?"

"Now, what did I tell you yesterday?"

"I know, but . . . I thought maybe you just had a bad day."

"No, I had a good day."

"But Mavis . . . Jesus. Don't you think this is a bit odd?"

"Yes, I do, but I also think it's serving a purpose, Al."

"Well, I don't get it. I really don't. If you want to be on *retreat*, Mavis, you don't have to stay in the *bathroom* all day. I go to the hospital six hours a day, you have the whole place to yourself. I'll tell you what. I'll call you before I come home. Then you can run right back in there before you see me."

She can't tell if he's angry or amused.

"Mavis?"

"Yes?"

"Did you hear what I said?"

"Yes, but I need to stay in here, Al."

"Well, then I'll be back after I eat dinner. I assume you're not making dinner again." A hopeful silence. She knows Al is leaning his better ear toward the door.

She sighs, waits.

Finally, "Fine," he says. She hears the door slam, the car start, and he is gone.

Mavis washes her face, brushes her teeth, then sits down at the edge of the tub with the box of Wheat Thins. She'd like a cup of coffee, she can smell it from Al having made it earlier. He doesn't usually drink all he makes. He usually sets her cup out, too, the Café Du Monde one they brought back from New Orleans. But if she goes out into the rest of the house, she'll lose what she's started here. She'll see dust on the coffee table, the morning paper lying messy on the kitchen table. The phone will ring, and she'll answer it. No. She will stay here.

When she has finished with the crackers, Mavis stores them

back under the sink. She puts on a clean pair of underwear, then her bra and slip. She wants to rinse her blouse, so she won't wear that quite yet. And if she's not wearing the blouse, why, what would the sense be in wearing the skirt? Or nylons?

She feels a prickle ascend her spine. She removes her bra, hangs it over the shower rod. Then she washes the blouse, drapes it next to the bra, and settles down into the tub with her note-book.

"Dear Eileen," she writes. "I know you're dead." And then she stops, stares straight ahead.

Outside, she hears a dog barking and the occasional sound of cars passing. A bush scrapes against the side of the house. It's the rose of Sharon they planted four years ago, loaded now with buds that will bloom in August as though in compensation for the cold that will follow. Mavis hates the winter, wonders every year why she stays in a place that is so cold. It's as though she has a stubborn belief it won't happen again, the astounding windchill, the air so cold it feels like sheet metal pressed up against your face when you step outside. She used to bundle the children up so hard for school they looked like pupae. "Hell, forget the cold, *you're* going to kill them," Al had told her. "They'll suffocate."

She stays in Minnesota, she supposes, because the fall is so beautiful. It sabotages her every year, makes her forget about what is to come. Last year, looking at the leaves when she was driving, she'd had an accident. She'd run into a lamppost on the side of the freeway, knocked it down. The car needed major repairs; she was unharmed; they were charged by the state for the cost of the lamp. "For Christ's sake, Mavis," Al had grumbled, paying the bill. "Keep your eyes on the road from now on, will you?" She had put a bowl of Wheatena before him, vowed out loud that she would, knew that she wouldn't. She couldn't help it, the leaves were so violently beautiful, and so short lasting. She wished the foliage would work in reverse, that you could see colors most of the time, the uniform green for only a few short weeks. But who could endure such richness? Surely people would go crazy from so much beauty. Or else they'd get used to it, and then ignore it, another form of craziness.

Mavis bites at her pen, looks at what she wrote, crosses it out. Well, she's not a writer. What in heaven's name did she think, bringing a notebook in here? She reaches up for her blouse, feels to see if it has dried at all. Not yet. Perhaps she could hang it out the window. She stands up in the tub, raises the window beside it. No. It won't work. Nothing to hang it on. Too bad there's no clothesline, she misses clotheslines.

She lies down in the tub again, crosses her ankles, closes her eyes, and a memory floats into her head like a dream. She is at a nightclub she and Al used to go to. They are dancing, Al in his good blue suit, she in her strapless white formal and satin high heels. She had just learned that afternoon that she was pregnant; and as Al held her close she whispered that the rabbit had died. Al had stopped dancing, held her slightly away from himself. Then, sick-looking with joy, he'd carefully escorted her back to their little round table with the lit lamp and the fancy glass ashtray holding gold-tipped matches. "I can still *dance*, Al," she'd said.

"Later, you can," he'd said. "After nine months." And then, "It is nine months, isn't it?"

She'd smiled yes.

"I all of a sudden didn't know!" he'd said. "I feel . . . Jesus, Mavis. A baby is in you!"

She'd nodded. "I know."

Later that night, after they'd gone to bed, Al had pulled her gently to him so that her back was against his chest. He'd raised her hair to kiss the back of her neck. "Mavis?" he'd said. "I think . . . I think you're a miracle. A kind of miracle." There was such reverence in his tone.

She'd turned to face him. "Everybody has babies, Al," she'd said, laughing, a little embarrassed.

"No."

"All right," she'd said, turning back over, letting him have it. She was twenty-five then. How can she be seventy-nine now? It occurs to her that she thought she would always be . . . oh, thirty-two. She would grow older, but she would be thirty-two. She could be *ninety*, but she would still be thirty-two; and she would set the table and all her family would come when she called, the children bumping into one another as they came through the kitchen door, Al following closely behind. His sleeves would be rolled up and he would be smiling, because he was hungry and dinner was there.

Mavis opens her notebook, then closes it again. She climbs out of the tub, gets an Orangina and a candy bar and the top library book, then climbs back in.

She hears Al come in the front door, checks her watch. Five-thirty. He couldn't have eaten already. He knocks at the door. "Mavis? You still in there?"

"Yes, I am."

"Well, I wondered . . . would you like to have dinner with me?"

"I can't come out, Al. I don't want to. I'm fine."

"Well, I know, but you have to eat. You must be starving."

"I've got food in here."

"What food?"

She is embarrassed to tell him. People's small passions, always embarrassing, she supposes. "Just . . . I've got things to eat, Al," she says.

"Well, you know, Mavis, I was thinking. If you did go away on a retreat, you'd go out to eat somewhere, right?"

She considers this. "Yes, I suppose so."

"And we'd be talking, too; if you went away, you'd call me, wouldn't you?"

"Well, of course I'd call you."

"So let's eat together, Mavis. Just pretend you're out to dinner and calling me."

"Now, you listen to me, Al, I'm getting pretty tired of telling you that I'm *doing* something in here! Oh, you just can't stand it that I'm not there all the time! You and Big Jim are just alike. If Eileen went to the corner mailbox, why, he'd have to come too. Otherwise he'd be at the window watching for her the whole time. Just like a little dog!"

"Wait a minute," Al says.

"What?"

"I meant, maybe . . . couldn't I come in there and eat with you?"

"Oh!" She sits down on the toilet seat, thinks. Then she says, "I don't think you'd like the food I have."

"I'll bring dinner," he says. "I got some stuff at the store. I'll *make* dinner."

"Well, I—" She stops, astonished. He has never once made dinner. "I think that would be very nice, Al."

"Okay. So I'll just go fix it now."

"All right. And Al? When you bring it in, could you bring me one of my dresses?"

"Your addresses?"

"No, one of my *dresses.* One of my summer *dresses.* I need something else to wear."

"Oh! Sure," he says, happily. And his happiness makes Mavis wonder if letting him in is the right decision. But when he knocks again and she opens the door to him holding a tray, her favorite blue shift lying across one of his arms, she is glad to see him.

"Come in," she says, stepping aside. What is this she is feeling, shyness? Can it be?

For his part, he has combed his hair—Mavis sees the careful wet lines when he sets their dinner down on the floor. The tray is covered with a dish towel. A surprise, then. He hands her the dress. "Here," he says. "Looks like you need this, all right."

She gasps, clutches at her chest, looks down at herself, embarrassed. She is still in her slip. "For heaven's sake," she says. "I forgot."

"Well." He lifts the towel. He has brought Chinese food: the plates hold chicken chow mein, rice, and egg rolls.

"Oh my," Mavis says. "Isn't this nice!"

Al points to the egg rolls. "You can buy these," he says. "Right in the grocery store. And then you just microwave them."

"Uh-huh."

"And of course, the chow mein, it's just in a can. Heat it right up."

"Right."

"The rice, I got at Chen's. Stopped on the way home."

"Well, it's all very good looking. Thank you, Al."

"Okay." He looks around. "Do we eat on the floor?"

"Oh." Mavis looks around as well, then puts the tray on the lid of the toilet. "Okay?"

They kneel on either side of the tray, sit back on their heels. "Not the most comfortable thing," Mavis says.

Al shrugs. "So. What have you been doing in here, Mavis?" He eyeballs the padded tub, the stack of magazines and books. "Reading?"

The egg rolls are still frozen in the middle. Mavis removes the bite she'd taken from her mouth, puts it on the side of her plate.

"You don't like it?" Al asks.

She smiles apologetically.

"Well, they were on sale," he says.

"It's okay."

"Chow mein's good, though, huh?"

"Oh, yes."

"So have you been reading, Mavis?"

"Well, I've mostly been thinking."

"About what?"

"About . . . whatever I want, Al. Do you know, it feels like I have never in my life been able to do that. It feels like I've been so . . . I don't know. Busy. Distracted. I just wanted to have a sense of . . ." She looks up at him, helpless to explain.

"Mavis, are you—" He puts his fork down, takes a breath in. "You're not thinking of leaving me, are you?" He leans slightly away from her, focusing, Mavis knows. His bifocals need replacing.

"No!"

"Well, I told someone about what you're doing. Harriet Bencher. And she asked were we having trouble. You know. And I said, well hell, I didn't think so. And *she* says, 'Al. Wake up and smell the coffee. Mavis wants to leave you. This is the first step.' I says, 'You're nuts, Harriet.' Which she is. But it got me thinking."

"First of all," Mavis says, feeling the heat of her indignation rise up in her neck, causing a sensation close to choking. "I have no idea in the wide, wide world why you would go and *tell* someone. Especially Harriet, who has such a big mouth." Harriet volunteers at the hospital with Al. Mavis has never met her and never wants to. "I don't see why this can't just be between you and me," Mavis continues. "It's just between you and me—and not even very much you!"

"I was scared, Mavis."

"Oh, you just couldn't wait to tell Harriet."

"I'm telling you I was scared! This is not normal behavior!"

She stands. "I'll tell you what, Al. I think I would just like you to go now."

He looks up at her.

"Yes. You just go on, now. I would like to be alone."

"Fine." He takes the tray, goes out the door, and she locks it behind him.

Two mornings later, Al comes to the door. "Mavis, you won't believe who's on the phone."

"I don't care who's on the phone. I don't want to talk on the phone." Though she and Al have made up—albeit with a door between them—she still does not want to talk on the phone. She and Al have come to an agreement. She will stay in the bathroom three more days; he will bring her whatever food and clothing she wants. Period.

But now he knocks again, saying, "It's the Chuck *Lokenvitz* show! You know? On channel thirty-seven?"

She stares at the door.

"Mavis?"

"I heard you. Very funny, Al."

"I'm not kidding, Mavis. I am not kidding you."

"Why would Chuck Lokenvitz be calling me?"

"Well, it's not Chuck himself, honey. It's a producer. That's how they do it. But someone must have called the show about you."

"Oh, they did. And I wonder who that someone could be. I just wonder who."

"It wasn't me."

"I know who it was. It was that damn Harriet."

"I suppose it might have been."

"You suppose!"

"Mavis, they're on the phone! The last guest that was on there went straight to *Oprah!*"

She opens the door. "I told you a million times we should get a portable!" She comes out into the hall, which, after four days in the bathroom, seems immense. She takes a few steps, then stops.

"Just take a message," she tells Al, and goes back into the bathroom. She closes the door, feels the return of a kind of safety.

"Take a *message?*" Al says.

"Yes. Tell them I'll be out in three days. I'll call them back."

"Mavis," Al says through the crack. "Mavis. It's the *Chuck Lokenvitz* show!"

"I don't care a thing about it," Mavis says, and sniffs. Where she has been, there is no Chuck Lokenvitz. Or Oprah Winfrey. There are her children, plumply young again, sitting in a busy circle in the sandbox and dressed in corduroy overalls and the tiny cardigan sweaters Eileen knit for them every Christmas. There is *The Ed Sullivan Show* on the little brown TV, all of the family watching, Ellie kneeling before Mavis so that she can have her hair put up in pink foam-rubber rollers. There is Eileen, sitting across from her at a booth in Woolworth's, sharing a piece of strawberry pie.

"Well, fine," Al says. "I'll just go tell the Chuck Lokenvitz show that you're much too busy to talk to them." And then, "You know I'm not kidding, right?"

"Yes, I know, Al," she says, and climbs back into the tub, unwraps her last candy bar. The hell with Chuck Lokenvitz.

Mavis's father was a mailman, delivered letters by horse cart at first. This is what she thinks about now, chewing the candy bar slowly, making it last. Her father changed into a baggy gray sweater and brown leather slippers every night when he came home, then sat at the kitchen table to listen to her and Eileen talk about school. He could sew better than their mother could, repaired all the girls' rips. He could sing like an opera star. He died of a stroke when he was sitting at that same kitchen table. "Whew," he'd said. "What a *head*ache I've got all of a sudden." And then he had neatly dropped dead, right before the astonished faces of Mavis, Eileen, and their mother. "For heaven's sake, Arthur," her mother had said at first. "Don't do that." And then, still holding her mixing spoon, she had bent over him and screamed, which neither of the girls had ever heard before. That was the worst part, that scream.

Mavis puts down the Heath bar, wonders how she'll die. That young rock singer, she choked on a ham sandwich. You just never know.

Once, when Mavis was out on a walk with Al, they'd seen an old man being pushed in a wheelchair by his young attendant. The man was so old, the blanket across his knees and his thick coat unable to hide his terrible thinness. The attendant was young and strong, his teeth white, and his smile fine and friendly. He'd nodded at Mavis and Al as they passed, and Mavis had taken Al's arm. "Al," she'd said, "if I ever end up in a wheelchair, will you push me outside? No matter how I look? I mean, look at that old man, it must make him feel better that he's outside, and that out here, nothing much has changed."

Al had stopped to pick a yellow wildflower. "Look at how pretty," he'd said.

"Will you, Al?"

"What, take you outside in a wheelchair? Sure."

"Okay," she'd said. "Don't forget."

He'd put the flower behind her ear, tenderly.

The moon comes out from behind a cloud, and the light pushes in through the bathroom window. Mavis turns on her side, away from it. She'd been thinking about Jonathan, about when he'd first learned to sit and was outside on the newly mowed lawn, blinking in the sun. The breeze was lifting up pieces of his baby hair, rearranging it on his perfect, round head. He'd picked up a blade of grass and put it in his mouth, and Mavis had leaped up from her lawn chair to take it away from him. Eileen, who'd been sunbathing with her—sunbathing and painting her toenails and eating ice cubes out of tall glass tumblers with her—had said, "Relax! A little grass won't hurt him." And years later, again, "Relax! A little grass won't hurt him," about the other kind. She was right, of course. Jonathan was fine. All the children were just fine, happy and healthy. Mavis opens her eyes wide. My God. It's true. They're all fine. She sighs deeply, closes her eyes.

Poochie died when she was very old, Mavis is thinking. Fourteen? Sixteen? But poor little Sassy, she was hardly over puppyhood.

Mavis is lying on the bathroom floor, doing leg lifts and trying to remember all the pets they've had. She's been getting leg cramps, and she thinks maybe exercise will help. Maybe it's good she's got only one more day. She heaves her legs up in the air again, remembers that once the kids brought home a dying baby rabbit they'd found under a bush. They'd begged Mavis to save it. She'd tried warm milk with an eyedropper and a heating pad, but the rabbit was too far gone. She gave the kids a fancy candy box she had been saving, told them they could bury the rabbit in it. They'd padded the box, still fragrant from chocolate, with toilet paper, then carefully laid the rabbit on top. Jonathan had wanted to tie the box shut, but Mavis had argued against it, saying it would spoil the look, and besides, the rabbit wasn't going anywhere. They'd dug a shallow hole in the backyard near the tomato plants, and she and the children had held hands around the burial site to sing "What a Friend We Have in Jesus." Then, at three-year-old Ellie's request, they sang "Here Comes Peter Cottontail." Ben was wearing his cowboy hat, and his holster was twisted around so that his jeweled revolver hung off his backside, an undignified sight at a funeral. Mavis remembers that she had wanted to adjust it, but didn't. She herself, after all, had been wearing the white apron with the big ruffles. A roast beef had been in the oven, she remembers that. She'd said, "I'm going to say a few words, kids, and then I've got to get back in there and finish dinner." Yes. She'd said exactly that. And the phone had been ringing when she came back in the house. My God, she remembers that, too. She'd washed her hands before she answered it. She can't remember who it was, though.

Mavis tries a sit-up, abandons it, returns to leg lifts.

They'd had seven parakeets. No, eight. Eight!

"You used to call them hoo-hoos," Mavis remembers Eileen saying. Eileen was in the hospital, one day after the surgery that took her breasts.

"Oh, I never did, either," Mavis said.

"You did too!" Eileen had raised herself up on one elbow, leaned toward Mavis to speak in a low voice. "You were five years old and we were in the bathtub together. And you were looking down at your chest, at your little boobs, pointing at them, and you said, 'This is my hoo-hoos.' And I started laughing, and you said, 'Well, what *do* you call them?' and I told you, 'Breasts.'" She'd taken a drink of water, then rearranged herself carefully against the pillows.

"Wait," Mavis said. "I do remember. Yes. You said it like this, real snotty: 'They are *called* breasts. B-r-e-a-s-t-s.'" And then she and Eileen had both started crying, Mavis a little harder than Eileen.

"You are not your breasts, you know," Mavis had said, reaching for Eileen's hand. "You're still you."

"I know," Eileen had said, her voice so small.

On her last night, Mavis puts the magazines in the garbage. She didn't read too much after all. She's written nothing other than the beginning of the letter to Eileen. She sits on the floor, back against the wall, drinks the last Orangina. She doesn't think she ever wants another one. When she comes out tomorrow and she and Al are sitting eating dinner, what can she tell him? How can she explain?

Al. Once, angry at him, she vowed to make a list of everything he did wrong. When it was long enough, she'd confront him. "Forty minutes late for dinner with not a word of apology," she'd written. "Spent our movie money on cigars." And then, when she was looking for a place in their desk to hide her list, she'd come across Al's will. "I am married to . . . ," the will had said, and there was a blank for him to fill in. "Mavis Elaine McPherson," he had written, in black penmanship far more careful than his usual. And she had regretted herself, had ripped the list up and flushed it down the toilet. Down this very toilet.

She stands, yawns, stretches. Well. What she wanted in here, she got. Uninterrupted time, to let thought lead to thought. She has enjoyed a rich kind of daytime dreaming that could only have come with the profound relaxation she has known here, she's sure of that. Something inside her has strengthened, too, though even now she cannot say exactly what it is.

She puts the empty bottle of Orangina in the case, stands to take off her dress and pull her nightgown over her head. She bends over the sink to wash, then looks up at herself in the mirror. Small drops of water cling to her face, and they seem beautiful to her. She dries off with the new pink towel Al brought her yesterday, thinking she'd appreciate a pretty one. "I am seventy-nine years old," she says, into the towel. And then, into the mirror, "And I have done everything right. And so did you, Eileen."

She turns out the light and starts for the tub, but then stops, goes instead out the door, down the hall, and into the bedroom. She can't see him at first, but feels his sleeping presence. She goes to her side of the bed, lifts the covers to slide in quietly beside him. She is thinking that all of life is accidental: the pink smudge of dawn, the depth of the oceans, the turning of the earth; everything, because everything that *started* everything was an accident, wasn't it? That's what they said. And so, one's own small life. What could you make of it? Who knew whom you would be born to, befriend, live out your life with? Those were accidents too, weren't they? Completely arbitrary things, barely noticed, most often. And yet.

She moves closer to Al, turns onto her side to put her arm around his wide middle. Couldn't there be just a bit of a grand plan, she wonders, maybe just a touch here and there; couldn't there be some benevolent intention that graced some lives?

"That's you, right, Mavis?" Al asks sleepily.

She closes her eyes, answers yes.

Departure from Normal

Every morning, Alice sits at the tiny kitchen table in her new apartment and reads the newspaper. She doesn't just glance at the front page like she used to. Now she has time, and she reads every single word. She is amazed at what she has been missing. There is accidental poetry, absurdist theater. Violence and comedy are separated by advertisements featuring women wearing brassieres and work skirts.

Alice saves the weather report for last, because she likes it best. She is intrigued by the "climate data," the obsessive care with which someone analyzes what happened last year compared with this year. She reads that today the departure from normal is +4 degrees. The departure this year is +277. She is unsure what the meaning of all this is, but in some way the larger number thrills her.

There are bold predictions in the weather forecast, no hemming and hawing: High today 80–85. Period. She likes that. There are childlike drawings of pointy-rayed suns and voluptuous clouds. There is a column of temperature listings for cities she's never seen. She reads that it is ninety in New Orleans and smells chicory; she reads seventy-four in San Francisco and sees wild-haired women hanging out laundry, the sheets fragrant and unwieldy and yanking at the lines. It is raining in Paris today: baguette wrappers wilt and soften with the humidity; taxis splash onto pants legs and leather shoes.

Alice likes to tell her story this way: First I got cancer. Then I got depressed. Then I got divorced. Then my parakeet got cancer. Then I got really depressed.

Alice has taken time off from work because she has had a recurrence, and she needs to decide what to do about it. She can try something experimental if she wants to. "Well. I'm very sorry," her doctors say. "Jesus," her friends say. Or, "Oh, *Alice*," they say. It has been so long since things were like they used to be. When a bad diagnosis comes, it is never how you think it will be, she tells people. It's the suddenness that's the problem. It is you, seasoning the pasta sauce and singing along with the radio. And then the phone rings and your doctor tells you he's gotten back some test results and can you come in to discuss them. Wait, you think. My rings still fit. My jeans. I just ate breakfast. I am thirty-six years old. In the middle, you see. The earth rotates while you speak, unmindful of the fact that you have just begun a quilt. You hang up the phone and start to learn.

After Alice reads the paper, she uses the weather report to line the bottom of the bird's cage. The bird is named Lucky. He is green and yellow, with tiny violet patches on his face. The violet looks the way blush does on women who can't see anymore—it is too dark, too low, ridiculous and endearing. He doesn't know he has cancer.

"You're going free today," Alice tells him. "It's going to be a beautiful day." The bird cocks his head, ruffles his feathers, and raises his wing, exposing his malignancy to her. It looks like a piece of cereal stuck onto him, she thinks. It looks like something she could just pluck off. She tried, once, when she saw it for the first time. It wouldn't come off, and the bird bit her. So she took him to the vet and the vet said it was cancer. Then he said, "Well, most birds live only six years. This one is seven." "Uh-huh," Alice said. She took the bird home, put a sheet around part of his cage, fed him a potato chip. She put him beside her while she lay on the sofa and looked at a magazine. She played the radio for him. Later, she let him fly around the house for hours, didn't push him off when he rode on her glasses.

Now she stands still, staring, fascinated by the bird's tumor. She has never seen her own. Is this the way her breast looked on the inside? The phone rings and she stands listening to it for a while. She picks it up, hangs up, and then leaves it off the hook. She finishes cleaning the cage, puts the bird in the sun, goes to shower.

She turns her back to the mirror to disrobe. She has never really looked. Before she was divorced, her husband looked. He looked right away, in fact, behaved remarkably, tried to kiss her where she never wanted to be kissed again. She had actually screamed in her humiliation, a startled kind of half cry, the kind of noise she made when she was badly frightened in a dream. She blushed then, wept, said it was too soon. He gave her time, he made excuses for her when it was past time. He brought home presents, silly and extravagant, he begged her to talk to him. She said, early on, "I don't get this. I can't make sense of this. I don't know what to do." And then she stopped talking. He seemed like a trick to her: staying the same and getting smaller; holding her tight and disappearing. "What do you want?" her friends would ask. "My God, Alice, what else can he possibly do?"

"I don't want anything," she said. But that was a lie. What she wanted was to be alone. And she told him that until he agreed and let her be alone. He still called sometimes; months after they were formally divorced he still said he was her husband.

Now Alice dresses in a sweatshirt and blue jeans. She remembers to comb her hair. Then she puts the birdcage in the passenger seat of her car and drives to the park. "Are you my buddy?" she asks Lucky as she drives. "Are you my friend?" He is silent, listening to her. "You and me, Lucky," she says. "We got the big one."

She sees no one when she pulls into the park. It is a workday, a school day, and too late for lunch. Everything is right. She walks along a jogging path, the cage clanging into her leg, the bird's water sloshing from side to side. When she is deep into the woods, she sits on a rock and puts the cage beside her, watches the bird for a while. He is excited, hops constantly from one perch to the other. "You're outside," she tells him, and rubs her finger along the bars of the cage. The bird can say words. He says his own name and, Alice believes, hers too. He whistles and makes soft, comforting sounds. But his wing doesn't lie flush against him anymore. And he has stopped eating almost entirely.

She opens the cage door. The bird hesitates, then hops closer. Alice speaks softly to him, holds her finger out to him. "Come on," she says. "You can go." Finally the bird steps onto her finger, and Alice pulls him out of the cage. He flies off immediately, lands on the branch of a nearby bush, chews excitedly at the leaves. Alice closes the cage door, puts her arms around herself, feels her eyes fill, her throat tighten. She watches for a while, as the bird flies from the bush to a tree and back again. He seems content to stay in the same area. Alice has imagined this scene so many times, and each time when she opened the door the bird flew immediately out of sight. And she was strong; she didn't cry. But now the bird stays near her and she isn't strong. She wants everything back from before—her old bird and her old self and her old life—and she feels the longing as an aching pressure that moves into her chest and steals her breathing. She lies down on the path, closes her eyes, and then opens them again to a piece of grass directly before her. It is arched delicately, weaving slightly in the wind. Ballet. As a child, she had loved this, lying in the grass and watching things close up. She saw bugs in alarming new ways; she saw canyons in pebbles. She liked especially the sudden reorientation that came with seeing her own hand again. Now she weeps softly, lets herself start to think about what she should do, wishes that a hand would open the door for her, because she is so tired.

She hears the sound of her bird above her, looks up to see his underbelly. He is low in the branches, chatting happily, making his whistling noises. She gets up and reaches out to pet him one last time, but he flies high up into the tree. He looks like jewelry. "Good-bye, Lucky," she says, and he chirps back in response to hearing his name. She picks up the cage and starts down the path. This is better than finding him dead on the bottom of the cage. It is better to get it over with now. She feels something land on her shoulder. It frightens her; she jumps, tries hurriedly to brush it away. But it is Lucky, squawking outrageously at her. He flies up to the top of her head to avoid her abusing hand. She holds her finger up to him, and when he sits on it, she puts him in front of her face. "Go!" she says, and flings him from her hand. But he circles around and comes back to sit on her shoulder. She begins walking. He'll take off in a minute, as he always does, she thinks.

But he doesn't. He stays on her shoulder until she again puts him on her finger. She opens the cage door, holds him up to it, and he goes in. He gets a drink, hops over to his mirror, and kisses himself.

Alice puts a piece of lettuce in Lucky's seed cup when she gets home. He ignores it. She turns on the radio and goes to lie down on her bed. Her hand picks up the phone and dials the number. Her voice says she wants to come home, and his voice says he will come and get her. It will be easy to pack. One cage, holding everything, and lined with a weather report that, despite what it pretends, knows nothing for sure.

Things We Used to Believe

Martha is lying in the grass, top of head to top of head, with her best friend, Alan. They'd had it in mind to watch the clouds pass and get pleasantly dizzy, but the sky is vacant, only blue. Alan is forty-nine and Martha is thirty-eight. She thinks sometimes that she would like to marry him but she is already severely married. Sometimes it just happens that you meet people in the wrong order.

They compensate in ways that will let them sleep nights: they discuss books over huge ice cream sundaes; they watch movies and hold hands in the dark under the camouflage created by the little pile of their jackets; they talk endlessly on the phone while they make dinners in their respective kitchens.

Today Martha is feeling the way your skin feels when the weather is just right—when it's not too hot, and not too cold, and there is no breeze whatsoever. It is a feeling of being inside something perfect, a feeling of very pleasant nothingness. "My mind feels like it's in absolute neutral," Martha tells Alan. He makes one of his deep, smooth sounds that implies agreement. Martha likes the sound, as she likes all the sounds that Alan makes. His voice comes out like silk or like velvet. The silk is usual, his old radio voice from the years that he was a disc jockey on a jazz radio show. The velvet is rare, and seductive, and irresistible, and it makes Martha nervous.

They are quiet for a long time, listening to the bold, irregular sounds of daytime life. It is one of the things Martha likes most about Alan that she knows his stomach will pull to the sounds of tiny children playing just as hers will. She also likes the way he always has a few fresh wildflowers on his kitchen table, gathered on his daily walks; and she likes the discrete, high-class way he uses a fork to squeeze lemon onto his fish. She asked him once to show her how, and he did.

Eventually, she breaks the friendly silence to say, "When I was a little girl, I thought that our appliances talked about us after we all went to bed. I thought they came into the kitchen and sat around talking about how they were treated."

Alan picks out a fat blade of grass and sucks on it as he contemplates what she has said. Then he says, "When I was a little boy, I thought Hawaii was off the coast of South Carolina. I was sure of it. I even lost money on a bet about it."

Martha smiles over at him. She thinks, I am so happy. She says, "I used to believe that after I'd gone to sleep at night, the blue fairy came into my room to paint stars on my ceiling. But if I woke up, everything would disappear. It was very frustrating."

Alan murmurs sympathetically. His voice is velvety now, and Martha feels punctured. She stirs a little, but says only, "I thought you could make yourself crazy by looking at your eyes really close up in the mirror."

"I thought that, too," Alan says. He is getting a little excited. "I also used to scare myself by saying over and over again, 'I am real. This is now.'"

"Did you try to imagine eternity?" Martha asks. "Did you try and try to imagine it until it made you cry?"

"Oh, sure," Alan says, in a serious and comfortable way, as though everyone did that.

Martha thinks of trying to have this conversation with her husband, Michael. If Martha told him something she used to believe, he might say, "Oh." Maybe he would say, "Oh." But probably he would look at her and say nothing. And if Martha asked, "Did you used to believe anything like that?" he would probably say, "I don't know. I don't remember." He would get irritated. And Martha would feel foolish for asking.

Now, though, she says, "I thought noodles grew on trees," and Alan laughs and says, "I thought bourbon tasted like warm root beer."

"I thought you made babies by rubbing palms together," Martha says.

"I love you," he says.

Martha is quiet for a moment, and then she rolls up onto her elbows to stare into his upside-down face. "I know," she says, and then he puts his hand on the back of her neck and puts her lips down precisely onto his. You would not think it possible to kiss easily with upside-down faces, but he has done it with all the efficiency and rarity of a hummingbird at the throat of a flower. It is a sweet, sweet kiss, full of meaning, the way that first kisses are; and it is scary, too, because of the knowledge that when the kiss is over, they will need to talk about what to do next.

Martha rises up from his face and lies back down. She thinks that her heart has moved up to be right beneath the skin on the surface of her chest, and that its wild rhythm must be visible. This is not true, of course, but she is revealed anyway, because of her breathlessness as she says unhappily, "Oh, Alan, what are we going to do?"

"Leave your husband, and marry me," he says.

"Right," Martha says. "Easy as pie." The face of her young son has appeared, enlarged, and moved deep inside of her. She sees herself last night, lifting him from the bath and onto her lap, wrapping the towel and then her arms around him. That smell. That perfect weight. She sees him later, sleeping, his thumb fallen halfway out of his mouth. Then she sees herself climbing into bed with Michael. Bitterness rises up in her like nausea; the grass starts to irritate her skin at the point of access between her jeans and her sweatshirt. She looks at her watch in order to emphasize her attachment to the real world. In forty minutes, she will pick Billy up from nursery school. They will make a cake together for dinner.

"Not as easy as pie," Alan says gently. He has raised himself up to look at her, this time right side up. "Not easy at all. But possible."

Martha looks away and wonders again how it can be that she is with Michael. A fortune-teller who once read her tarot cards told her, looking up with a kind of amazement on her face, "You don't *feel* married."

"You're right," Martha said. She stared hard at the fortune-teller, then defused the moment by looking down and pointing to another card, saying, "What does that one mean?"

"It says you have a beautiful imagination," the card reader said, and Martha said, "Ah."

Martha starts to sigh and ends up with a low growl of frustration. "Let's not even get into this," she says. "You know I can't leave. I can't." And then, again, "I can't."

Crows caw in the distance. Someone honks a car horn three times. They are impatient. They mean business. Martha gets up onto her knees and pushes grass off herself. "Let's go," she says. "Let's go somewhere."

Alan lies still, doesn't move. "Nope. I'm not done."

Martha is wary, distressed, but here is all he says: "I used to think whenever the radio played a song, the performer was right there at the station. I thought the bands were just all lined up, waiting for their turns. I wondered how they could break down and set up so quickly."

Martha says, "I thought cats had no eyelids. I also thought the sexiest thing in the world to do was to put on a pair of high heels and dangle a cigarette from your lips, in front of a mirror. I did it quite a lot when I was nine."

They get up, and she sees that his sneakers are huge. She understands that there is much about him that is unfamiliar to her. They start walking toward the lake. They walk to keep from the bedroom, where things would only get more difficult.

"Step on a crack, you'll break your mother's back," Martha says, avoiding all the lines on the sidewalk. Alan jumps up high and lands directly on one. Martha gasps, covers her mouth. "You are *bad*," she says.

He stares straight at her, his love surrounding him like an aura. "So are you," he says.

"So am I," she agrees.

Caretaking

I am five years old, lying outside on a blanket. The sun is spring-time warm, there is a delicate breeze, and the combination is an opiate. I want to suck my thumb, though I have been told lately that I must not. But it is all that is missing to make the moment flawless, and so, with my head turned away from the house, I raise my arm up slowly to slide my thumb home. Ah. It tastes properly salty; and the cool smoothness of its surface is perfection. I sigh out my nose. I rub my tongue against the familiar bump of my thumb's knuckle, deeply content. I am almost given over into sleep when I hear my mother's voice coming from the second-story bedroom window. "Uh-uh!" she calls. "Don't suck your thumb!" It is a gentle, singsong reprimand. I am humiliated into wide-awakeness, and decide to abandon the blanket for some-thing else, a place that suggests no carnal transgressions. But first I must know how my mother knew—how did she know I was sucking my thumb? I stand up to ask her. She is still leaning on her elbows out the window, admiring the day. She is wearing her housecleaning kerchief, and she looks beautiful. She has naturally curly black hair, and always when she wears her kerchief a few strands of it escape and misbehave engagingly around her face. She wears red lipstick and no other makeup, and when she smiles she reveals two deep dimples that I envy so much that when I think of them I feel a little ill. I have tried to make some for myself, to no avail. I have corkscrewed my index fingers into the hated plain pads at the sides of my face at regular intervals during the day. I have taped marbles into them at night. No dimples yet. I trust that when I am older a reliable dimple-inducing method will come to me. For now, I put my hand on my hip and shade my eyes from the sun to yell up at my mother, "How did you know?"

She smiles down at me with her terrible dimples. "What?" Her voice seems borne by the breeze, carries far, stays alive for a long time—it is just that kind of day, perfect for thumb sucking. Angered by a new surge of desire, I ask again, irritably, "How did you know?"

"Oh," she says. "Well, a pixie told me."

I look around uneasily. I don't see any trace of her. "How did *she* know?"

My mother has remembered her work, and she is pulling back into the house. "She watches you," she tells me, and disappears.

I sit on my blanket, disgruntled. I wonder if this pixie also knows what I am thinking. Oh, it can't be.

Last week when I came to see my mother, she was wearing a housecleaning kerchief as in the old days, covering her now silver hair. Her dress was buttoned one button off, and she was wearing only one slipper. I found the other one on top of the stove. My stomach lurched. "Mom," I said, as gently as I could, "why is your slipper here?"

She stared at it blankly. "Why, I don't know." A robin came into the tree near the kitchen window where we stood. My mother saw him and said, "Oh, look. Look at his fat orange breast."

We sat at the little kitchen table with the embroidered table-cloth and I asked what she'd had for breakfast. She traced a blue daisy with her fingertip and began to cry. "I don't remember. Ask your father." My father died four years ago. On his last day, he was fixing a stuck wheel on my son's bicycle. He clutched his chest, my mother later told me, looking quite surprised. Then he stared at her, sitting in her lawn chair a few feet away from him, and, with a look of extreme clarity and love, neatly died. She dropped the peas she'd been shelling onto the ground and never let anyone pick them up. For a whole year after my father's death, you could still find some, if you looked carefully enough.

Now, I said what I'd imagined saying for nearly a year. I said, "Mom, I'm worried about your living here alone. I think you need other people around."

She gasped. "Oh, no. I don't want to go to a nursing home. There are some things worse than dying, and that's one of them." She began to cry in earnest then, and clutched my hand with both of hers. "Oh, please," she said, shaking her head and squeezing my hand so hard it hurt.

Over her badly buttoned dress she was wearing a blue print apron featuring various types of kitchen paraphernalia. Spatulas, knives, wall clocks, and mixing bowls floated dreamlike across her bosom, down her back. She reached into the pocket for a wadded-up Kleenex. I wished hard for the first time in my life for a brother or a sister—this was too hard for one person. I went over to her and held her against me, and she stopped crying. We were both still, waiting. "Mom," I said finally, to the delicate part on the top of her silver head. "Please just come home with me tonight. Stay over. Joey would love to see you—he got his first high school report card yesterday. We'll have a nice dinner."

She twisted her wedding ring on her hand, and I hoped she wouldn't say again to ask my father. She didn't. She stood up and said she would get her purse and overnight bag. She seemed full of dignity and pleasant anticipation now—we might have been going to the opera. "Would you help me with my coat?" she asked when she reappeared in the kitchen. I said that I would, but asked if she would like to take her apron off first. "For heaven's sake," she said, looking down at herself and laughing. "Holy buckets."

I am seven, riding in the backseat of the car while we take a trip across country. It is summer, and it feels as though we will all be free of obligation forever. We drive until we are distracted by something, and then we stop. We eat in restaurants with place mats that are maps, with stars for cities. They tell us where we are, and we trace on them where we think we'll go, though we are never definite. My father is irresponsible when it comes to filling up—it is my mother who always notices that we are almost out of gas. "Holy buckets, Fred," she says. "Find a gas station, will you?" And we do, always just in time, and then while my father does the manly thing and stands by the car to chat with the attendant, my mother and I go to "freshen up," as she calls it. In the almost air-less, tiled bathroom, we deliberate in front of the vending machines. I am allowed one thing. Sometimes it is an Ace comb in a black plastic holder. In the finest places, there are things like tiny dolls in baskets, or twin Scottie dogs on a gold chain. I am also fond of little tubes of toothpaste.

When I am tired, I stretch out on the backseat to stare at the constant blue sky through the rear window. Sometimes I hear my father ask my mother to rub his shoulders and neck, which embarrasses me. I hear them talk adult talk, tell stories with endings I don't understand. Sometimes I pretend I am asleep and hope that they will talk about me, and often they do. They tell each other tales of various achievements of mine; or they express admiration for what they insist are my good looks; or they recount things I've said that they found amusing. I must be careful not to smile with them.

I like the monotonous drone of the tires on the pavement, the containment in one small space of everything I need in my life. I will be safe forever—I can tell by the simple sight of the back of my parents' heads. They are up: alert, careful, and making the right decisions. I can stare into the sky until I sleep for real, worryless.

When we arrived at my house, my mother saw Joey first. He was coming down the sidewalk from school. "Well, that's Joey, isn't it?" she asked.

"Sure is." I called to him to help me unload groceries.

Joey greeted his grandmother hesitantly. He was uncomfortable around my mother lately because he found her newly unreliable. At thirteen, his fear of embarrassment was acute, and he knew that at any given moment my mother might do something to make him quite uncomfortable—astounded, even. "She's wacked out now," he'd recently said, petulantly, and I had angrily sent him to his room. Later, I sat on his bed and apologized. "I feel bad for her," I'd said. "It makes me really angry to hear you talk about her that way."

He sat at his desk and spun his globe around. "But all I meant is that she's *changed*," he said. "That's true, isn't it?"

They are going out for the evening to someplace very special. My father wears a suit and looks proper but boring. My mother, though, wears her white formal that lives in a zippered plastic bag in her closet. It has what I believe are diamonds all across the bodice. I have spent much time standing in my mother's closet so that I may be close to such a wondrous thing. Once, I unzipped the bag to rub my hand against the diamonds.

My mother comes down our long staircase with the dress floating around her as though it is alive, and with her hair in a French twist. She is wearing rouge tonight. I stare at her, my mouth dry with admiration. I want to tell her how wonderful she looks. "Here comes the bride," I say. She touches my cheek, and I smell her perfume. "Thank you," she says. Her voice is so gay, so full of life. At parties she is always in some large group of people, making them laugh, making them like her. When I am introduced to my mother's friends, they tell me they hope I'll be just like her. I stare up at them while I shake their big adult hands, muted by my fervent longing—can't they see?—to do just that.

Joey took three bags and my mother told him how strong he was. He shrugged. "They're light."

Inside, while I unpacked the bags, my mother and Joey sat at the kitchen table together. "You look pretty good, Gram," Joey said. "How've you been?"

"Well, I've been just fine," she told him. "Of course, I can't do what I used to do."

He looked down at the table. "No."

"But I get along. I'm here for dinner," she added.

"Oh yeah? That's nice."

My mother opened her purse and took out a tube of lipstick. She pursed her lips and applied it slowly. It was wildly off the mark. Then, staring straight ahead, she began to sing and to keep time by slapping the table gently with the palm of her hand. I saw Joey shift his weight uncomfortably on his chair. "Well," he said, "I've got a lot of homework." He was begging me, in his way.

"Go ahead up to your room," I told him. "We'll see you at dinner."

Joey is three, and having a tantrum. He doesn't want to leave my mother's house. "No!" he screams. "I want to stay here! I love *Grandma!*" I pull him outside with me, while he protests with wails that escalate in direct proportion to his distance from her side. "You can come *back*, Joey," I hear my mother say. "I'm not going anywhere!"

My husband came through the door into the kitchen and saw my mother. "Oh—Peg!" He put down his briefcase to hug her. "How are you?"

"I came for dinner."

"Uh-huh. Good. I haven't seen you for a while."

My mother chewed her lip. "Oh?"

Jim paused. "Well, I mean, what's it been? Couple weeks or so?"

She looked bewildered. "Well, I just don't know."

Jim put his hand on her shoulder. "It doesn't matter—I'm just happy to see you." He turned to me. "Want me to start the grill?"

I nodded yes. I thought she was worse. Every time I saw her, I thought she was worse.

We ate in silence, for the most part. Joey showed my mother his report card at my request, and seemed happy when she said, "Why, Joey! This is excellent! I believe you're even smarter than your mother was!" But then during the course of the meal she asked three times what the salad was. I can't stand this, I thought, as I cut my steak into unnecessarily small pieces. I thought of Jim's suggestion to put her into a home of some kind. "There are some good ones," he'd said. "I think we can afford it. But I just don't think it would work if she lived here. I mean, do you?"

I am nine, swinging from the clothesline pole, kicking my legs to make myself higher and higher. Suddenly, I slip off and land flat on my back on the concrete below. I stand up and realize that I cannot breathe. I am terrified, and run into the house. My mother is on the telephone, but she says, quickly, "I'll call you back," and hangs up. I run into her arms, thinking myself a baby but thinking also that I am dying. And then my breathing comes back. I take in huge gulps of air and sob, "I thought I was dying! I couldn't breathe!"

My mother pulls me down onto her lap. "I am too old to do this," I say into her shoulder, humiliated but comforted.

She hugs me tightly. "You will never be too old for this," she tells me. "Don't you know that I will always take care of you?"

After dinner, I took my mother into the guest room. "I forgot a nightgown," she said. I told her she could use one of mine. I gave her towels, some she had given me. "Aren't these nice—wherever did you find such pretty towels?" she asked, and I thought she could be teasing me. And she was. "Don't I have good taste?" she asked, and smiled.

We talked in the living room after we'd both changed. "Mom," I began, in what I hoped was a very reasonable tone of voice. "It's hard to live alone, isn't it? Wouldn't it be nice for you not to have to worry about making your own meals or doing your own cleaning? There are residential communities, you know, that aren't really nursing homes."

She looked down. "I would like to stay in my own house."

I sighed, angry. "Look, I know you would. But it's just not safe anymore, Mom. You had a *slipper* on top of your stove, right next to a burner!"

She frowned at me. "I did not."

It wasn't going to work to try to talk her into anything. When she was diagnosed, I was given power of attorney. Now was the time for me to be her caretaker. I changed the subject. "What have you been reading?" I asked her, and she stared at me, silent. "Mom?"

"Oh, I don't read," she said. "Never have."

I am fresh out of the bathtub, dressed in clean cotton pajamas and a red chenille robe with big silver buttons that I believe to be quite sophisticated. My mother has combed out my hair, a gruesome ordeal for both of us, and my reward for not complaining is my clown book. My mother puts on her reading voice and though we have heard the book one hundred times, we enjoy it again, both of us. At the end, a clown pops up. I admire most about him his extraordinary red hair. I fold him carefully back inside, and then put the book back in its special place, the far right-hand side of the lowest shelf on the bookcase. I whisper good night to it and gently caress its deteriorating spine. I love my books passionately, as does my mother. She reads in her bed every night following a certain protocol: She props herself up on two pillows. Then, while she reads at an astonishingly rapid rate, she slowly eats one piece of fruit and one candy bar, believing that one makes up for the other. She usually picks apples as the fruit, and a Mars or Heath bar for the candy. I believe that these candy bars are for adults only, and I aspire to someday being able to lie in my own adult bed with my own adult books and eat them. My mother never reads just one book at a time—my father complains about books all over the nightstands. They have fallen on him in the middle of the night. Sometimes they have replaced him. Often, my mother stays up much too late reading, and then she is tired in the morning when she makes my breakfast. "I just couldn't stop," she tells me.

"I'm going to bed, Mom," I told her. "I'll see you in the morning."

When Jim climbed into bed beside me he said, "It's so sad. I don't know what to tell you. Maybe she should live here."

I stared out the window. "I don't know. I don't know! I mean, think of how it would be. She's getting worse all the time. Last week her car was parked in the middle of the street with the keys still in it. And remember how I told you about how her pot holders were scorched? Today she had a *slipper* on top of her stove! What if she starts a fire?" Jim reached for my hand. I sighed. "Sometimes I think about all these floating spirits in heaven, like new recruits. They're deciding whether to come to earth and be human. As the last part of their orientation, they get to look down and see life in progress, see how it'll go. And they really see it— the diseases, the accidents, the utter arbitrariness of it all, and then the inevitability of death. Oh, it's awful, when you think about it, isn't it? Still, I think that seeing that, all those spirits would want to come anyway." I paused for a moment, and then added, "And I would, too."

Jim said, "I would say, 'What? You mean, that's how it is? You just go slogging through life only to die?' "

"So you'd pass, huh?" I asked him.

"Hell, no," he said. "I'd probably push to be first in line." Then he reached for me in tender hopelessness and I stared over his shoulder and said, "I don't understand anything."

"Nobody does." He held me tighter.

I had been asleep for a while when I heard a loud noise coming from downstairs. It took a while for it to register that it was the front door slamming. I ran to the window and saw my mother outside in her slip, walking purposefully down the sidewalk. I put on my robe and went after her. She startled when she heard me call her. "Oh, you scared me!" She laughed.

"Mom," I began, out of breath. "Mom." I couldn't think of anything to say. I began to cry.

"Why, darling, what's the matter?" she asked, and suddenly I wanted only for her to be my mother again. I wanted to tell her what the matter was, and I wanted her to fix it. Instead, I said, "Let's go in the backyard."

We sat in two lawn chairs, facing each other. The night was warm, beautiful. I showed my mother the full moon, and she smiled appreciatively and lifted her face up to it. Then I said, "I love you, Mom, and I want to keep you safe. You can't live by yourself anymore, so we'll find you a place where you won't be alone. I'll do everything I can to help make you happy there."

She was still, listening to me. "I know this is difficult," she said. And then, softly, "I know I'm ill."

"Do you, Mom?"

"Oh yes, I know. Sometimes I forget—do you know?"

"I know, Mom. It's part of the disease."

"It's Alzheimer's disease."

"Right."

"And where is Joey? And Jim?"

"They're asleep, Mom."

"Oh, are they?"

"Yes, it's—well, it's late."

"Oh. I wondered." She turned to me then, and her eyes were not clouded or confused, and she looked glorious in her slip. "Well, you know I love you too, of course," she said. I nodded, two parallel lines along my throat aching. "And I trust you. I'll go where you say." She looked around the yard. "Such lovely flowers," she said. "I wish they would last forever."

Her voice seemed so small in the pale darkness of the night, against the infinite number and complicated history of the stars in the sky above us. I moved closer and put my arm around her, as though I could protect her. As though I could save us both.

Sweet Refuge

When I was a visiting nurse, I got a reputation for liking the hard patients. So when a case came up involving a man with cancer of the pancreas who was "difficult to manage," he was assigned to me. He was being sent home from the hospital to die, and he needed someone to do dressing changes on his chest catheter, to help him with his morphine pump, and to provide emotional support. He was extremely angry, they said. Mean. Did I want him? And I said yes, because an immediate alliance had been struck between that patient and me as soon as they told me he was angry: he was thirty-one years old.

I went to the hospital to meet Richard the next day. One of the floor nurses led me to his room, talking in a low voice about how I could expect very little in the way of cooperation. "Sometimes he simply refuses to speak," she said. "Don't be surprised."

We entered his room as he was emerging from the bathroom. A haze of marijuana smoke hung suspended in the air behind him. "Oh yes," the nurse told me quietly. "He also smokes a lot of dope." She spoke up then, told Richard, "This is Abby. She'll be seeing you at home."

I smiled, held out my hand. "Abby Epstein," I said. "Nice to meet you."

He didn't take my hand. He walked over to his bed, sat on it, and stared out the window. He was heartbreakingly thin, but still quite handsome, a light-skinned black man with wire-rimmed glasses.

"I'll just leave the two of you alone to get acquainted," the nurse said. She rolled her eyes at me, then left the room.

I moved over to stand in front of Richard, cleared my throat. "I just wanted to say hello, and to tell you that I'll be coming to see you every day."

Nothing.

"I wondered if eleven o'clock would be a good time." He looked up at me, then away. "It could also be ten," I said. "Or twelve."

Nothing.

I waited. I heard the dripping of the bathroom faucet. The dope smell was still thick in the air. I wondered who sold it to him, what their conversation had been. *I'll give you a discount, man. I mean, you're checking out, right?* I shifted my weight, bent down a little to try to look into his face, but he turned away. "Well, I won't take any more of your time now," I said.

He laughed. "Yeah. I'm pretty busy."

"I'll see you tomorrow at eleven."

I was almost out the door when I heard him speak again, but I couldn't quite make it out. "Pardon?"

He looked me slowly up and down. "Fuck. You."

I took in a breath, breathed back out. "I'll see you tomorrow, Richard."

When I was a freshman in college, I worked weekends at a hospital cafeteria. My job was to push a heavy steam cart up to a little kitchen where I'd dish out meals for the patients on that particular unit. The nurses lined up to carry the trays to the patients. At that time, they still wore little white caps, each different from the other, and stud earrings. They wore their hair up off their collars. Their uniforms were white, their stockings were white, their shoes were white, even their watchbands were white. They were always busy, but they were remarkably cheerful. I admired them: their understated makeup, their calmness in the face of ever-impending disaster, their absolute willingness to help. I had gone to school intending to become a teacher, but after watching the nurses for a few weeks, I decided to change my major. "I'm going to go to nursing school," I told one of the nurses, and she said, "Good. We need you."

After I graduated, I got my own white cap with a navy blue stripe. I thought it looked great. I used white bobby pins to anchor it and I wore white pearl studs. I was cheerful, like my mentors. And I worked happily in hospitals until the time my husband picked me up after work one night and complained, again, that I hadn't come out on time. "I was pushing on someone's chest," I said. "I was making his heart pump so he wouldn't die. It didn't particularly matter that my shift had ended."

My husband stared straight ahead, shifted the car too precisely.

By the time we could afford two cars, I'd had children and needed to be home more often. So I started working part-time, visiting patients in their homes. As it happened, I liked doing that even more than working in hospitals. Because I saw all of those patients. They weren't stripped of themselves, sitting alone in a hospital bed with a wrinkled patient gown tied on them. Now they wore their own clothes and sat in their own chairs, surrounded by the things that made them themselves: their newspapers and coffee mugs, their exuberant dogs and various family members, their pictures on the walls. I liked that I could check their temperature while I smelled their dinner cooking, that I heard their phones ringing, saw their gardens blooming. I liked being closer to them. That's what is best about nursing: you get close to patients, because when people are sick, they don't bullshit. They are real, and you can be real back. What I understood about myself the day I decided to become a nurse is that there's nothing I prize more than looking into someone's eyes and seeing them true. I thought if I were a nurse, I could do that over and over again.

Richard lived in a brick building with six apartments. It was an old place in fairly good shape, with high, interesting windows and gigantic screened-in porches. I stood outside looking at the place, wondering what he'd thought when he first saw it. Probably he didn't think, *So this is where I'll die.* Probably he thought, *This will do for now.*

I rang number five and was surprised to be immediately buzzed in. I was afraid I'd have to get the super, that Richard might refuse to admit me, but when I reached his door, I saw why I'd been let in so promptly—someone else had done it. A red-haired woman, pale and beautiful and wary looking, held out her hand. "I'm Richard's girlfriend," she said. "Laura."

I shook her hand, told her my name. "Is he up?" I asked.

She motioned me inside the living room. "Yes, he's in the bedroom. He's lying down. You're going to do his dressing, right?" I nodded. She sat down on the sofa, lit a cigarette. "I was taught how, you know; but he doesn't like for me to do it." She exhaled in a straight line, up into the air over her head. There was some anger in it. Then she looked levelly at me. "I thought I'd watch, though, if you don't mind."

"I don't mind at all," I said. "You can help me if you want."

"No," she said. "Richard wouldn't like it."

"I need to do an interview first," I said. "First-visit stuff—just some routine questions."

"He won't tell you anything."

I hesitated, then said, "Well, maybe I'll just try."

She shrugged. "Call me when you're ready for me."

She was wearing a pair of tight blue jeans and a white blouse, knotted at the waist. Her feet were bare, her toenails painted a deep red. She wore large gold hoop earrings and her hair was in a falling-down bun that was lovely. There were violet-colored smudges under her eyes, and I wondered when she'd last slept through the night. When was the last time she'd worried over something at work, over the cost of groceries? What luxury most of us enjoy, complaining about the things we do: long lines, uncomfortable weather, the numbers on the bathroom scale. I couldn't imagine being Laura, waking up at night to someone you loved and knew was dying. Surely she watched, sometimes, in the moonlight, for the rise and fall of his chest. Surely she rose up on one elbow, full of fear, to look; then fell, relieved and aching, back onto her own pillow. Usually people die at night, late. Three A.M., four-fifteen. They are being polite, I suppose. They mean not to grieve everyone so much.

I thought about when Laura went with Richard to hear about what was wrong with him. I knew they'd been told in his doctor's office, with its pale colors and diplomas on the wall and pictures of the doctor's children tanned and smiling. I saw them hearing the news and then getting back in their car, very different people from the ones who'd left it an hour ago. They'd locked their doors. Things would never be the same. They'd buckled their seat belts. Things would never be the same. What anguish there is in knowing that things will really never be the same! Once, when my daughter was seven, I came into her room to tell her dinner was ready. She was standing at her window, looking out at the sunset. "Time to eat," I said. And she said, not turning around, "There will never be another day exactly like this one ever, ever again." I only swallowed, full of a mother's regret for the necessary lessons of childhood. I only said, "It's fried chicken, honey. Wash up."

"Who is it?" I heard Richard yell. Laura stood, ground out her cigarette. "Wait here," she told me. She went into the bedroom and I heard her say, "It's the nurse. The one who came to the hospital to see you yesterday." There was a silence then, and Laura came out and nodded. I wasn't sure, suddenly, and I stood there until she said, "Go ahead. He's waiting."

The bedroom was dark, filled with bookshelves. The one over Richard's head held hardback volumes about theater. I looked at them quickly, then at him. "Are you the one interested in theater?"

His look was one of contempt and astonishment mixed. He was lying on a bed that had been neatly made. There was a beautiful quilt, rose colors and greens, folded back at his feet. He pulled up his T-shirt to reveal his dressing. "Do it," he said.

"Well, I need to ask you some questions first. I have to take this . . . sort of . . . health history." In my armpits, I felt the deep tickle of perspiration starting. I opened my bag to pull out his chart.

"I'm dying," he said. He meant that was all I needed to know.

I looked at him. "I know. And I need to tell you that I don't have any particular way of being about that, Richard. I know it's unfair what's happened to you. I know you have a lot of pain. We can talk about it, if you want to. But I come in here and I see your books and my inclination is to try to get to know other parts of you. There are still other parts to you."

He looked around me, yelled, "Laura!" She came into the room and he gestured angrily toward me. "Get her out of here."

She sighed. "Richard—"

"Get her the fuck out."

"Fine," she said. "Then I'll do your dressing."

"No, you won't." He struggled to sit up.

"Look," I said. "I'll do it. I'm sorry, Richard, if I offended you. I'll do your dressing and that's all for today, okay? I'll just do it and go. All right?"

He sat, swaying slightly from side to side, as though remembering a dance. I noticed the scent of lilacs coming through the open bedroom window, that bold, little girls' perfume smell. I regretted myself, my too rapid move toward an unearned intimacy. After a moment, though, Richard lay back down, closed his eyes, and pulled up his shirt. I nodded at Laura, and she stood back, leaned against the doorjamb. I worked quickly, quietly. I finished in seven minutes. I said, "I'll see you tomorrow, same time," and left the bedroom.

Laura followed me to the front door. "I'm sorry. He's not himself."

"Oh well, how can he be?"

She smiled, a weary thing. "You know, three weeks ago, he was jogging every day. Five miles. He did real well for a whole year after he was diagnosed. But all of a sudden . . ." She looked down, then raised her head back up. "This shouldn't be a surprise. But it is anyway. I feel like I'm going crazy. I really feel crazy." She opened the door, sighed quietly. "See you tomorrow."

I walked down the steps. They creaked. And I thought, *Richard won't hear this anymore. He'll never walk down these steps again.* But I was wrong.

Ida Brazinsky lived with her boyfriend, Frankie, in a falling-down duplex in Chelsea. Most of the time they sat at the kitchen table watching a tiny black-and-white TV and drinking whiskey. I knew Ida was seventy-four, and I put Frankie at several years older, although when people set about ruining themselves at an early age, it's hard to tell. I'd stopped at a convenience store for something quick to eat, and the only thing that looked decent was a shrimp cocktail—the kind in a little glass, with a white under-the-sea motif painted on the sides. I asked Ida for a church key and a fork, so I could eat before I examined her. "Oh, sure," she said, and shuffled over to where she kept the silverware. I saw something streak out of the way of the light when she opened the drawer. I wanted to ask her if I could rinse the things off before I used them, but I didn't want to hurt her feelings. I needn't have worried—Ida washed them off herself, muttering, "Goddamn roaches!" Then she handed the utensils to me.

"Take your time," she said kindly, and Frankie roared, "Pull up a chair, for Christ's sake!" He was already drunk; he leaned uncertainly toward the left. He watched me eat. I smiled at him a little after every bite.

Wrestling was on; two impossible-sized men circled each other like dogs intent on an introduction. Ida was glued to the action. "I love that one," she said, pointing. "He's my boyfriend." She fingered the pink foam-rubber roller above her ear. This got Frankie's attention for a moment. "*I'm* your goddamn *boy*friend!" he said. "*I'm* the one sits here with you every goddamned day!"

"Oh, Frankie." Ida smiled and waved her hand at him in a way that was—you could see it—flirtatious. And she had her head down, blushing a little. I have admiration for people who can take tenderness where they find it. I excused myself and went to wash my hands in Ida's bathroom. As usual, she had laundry hanging to dry on a wooden rack that she kept in the tub. There were several pairs of her underwear, all the size of sails, and there were some of Frankie's, too, stained hopelessly but draped with care next to hers. Sometimes the door to Ida's bedroom was open and I would see that the covers were pulled back, and I'd think about them sleeping together, uttering boozy, outrageous words of love to each other. I have to say this: I think Ida was happy.

When I came back to the table, Frankie was holding my empty shrimp cocktail glass, turning it around and around. He looked up at me, one eye squinted against the brightness coming from the window. "Can I have this?"

Ida inhaled sharply. "Frankie! That's a *fancy* glass! I'm sure she wants it for herself!"

"Oh, *no!*" I said, and then, seeing their two sets of eyes, blue and trusting, on me, I said, "I mean, yes, it is a very nice glass. It's perfect for juice in the morning. But I have so many already, and I'd be pleased for you to have that one."

"Well . . . ," Ida said doubtfully.

Frankie leaned onto the table, then pulled himself up. "I'll wash it real good," he said. "Then I'll let my girl have a drink out of it."

I pulled my stethoscope out of my bag. "Let me listen," I told Ida, and she pulled down the neckline of her faded floral housedress. She had doused herself with dusting powder, a well-intentioned gesture that had failed.

"What's it singing today?" Ida asked, winking, smiling at me. Her dentures were out. I hoped she hadn't lost them again.

"It's singing 'Peg o' My Heart,'" I told her. "Sounds good. Your heart rate is fine, Ida. Slow and regular. Real good. You've been taking your pills, haven't you?"

"I make her!" Frankie said. "I remind her every morning!"

"He does," Ida said. "The old fart."

I listened to Ida's lungs, felt her ankles for swelling, checked her blood pressure. Then I left her and Frankie watching wrestling and sharing Four Roses out of the shrimp cocktail glass. They were yelling at the blond man on the screen for using an illegal hold. "That ref is fucking *blind!*" Frankie said, and Ida agreed with him. "Fucking blind," she said, and took a ladylike sip.

That night when my husband and I were in bed, I told him about visiting Richard. "I feel like I blew it," I said. "I pushed him too hard. He's not ready to talk to me."

"I don't know why you think you need to get so involved," John said. "I'm sure he has people he talks to. Why does he have to open up to you?"

"I just . . . I feel like I do a better job if I know someone."

"How much time does he have left?"

"His doctor thinks a couple of weeks, maybe."

He nodded. "So forget the psychotherapy. Just go and do what you're supposed to do."

"It's not psycho*therapy*." I turned out my light, turned on my side, away from him.

"Well, what would you call it? What is it, then?"

I breathed in, closed my eyes. "I don't know. I just need to see him. To know him as something more than a patient with cancer of the pancreas who's dying."

"*Why?*"

I turned toward him, looked at him. "You know what? I have been married to you for fifteen years. And sometimes I think, *Who the hell are you?*"

He turned out his light, turned over.

"Good night," I said.

Nothing.

Richard was up, sitting on the sofa and watching television. He nodded at me when I came in the room. "Ready?" I asked.

"In a minute." He leaned back, picked up the remote, and turned off the television. "What's your name, again?"

"Abby."

"Abby." He stared at me unsteadily. I realized he was stoned. "You know what Abby means in Hebrew?"

"No."

"Means 'sweet refuge.'" He said it slowly, nearly seductively, watching my face.

I smiled. Nodded. "Uh-huh."

"Did you know that, Abby? Did you know that you mean 'sweet refuge'?"

"No," I said. "That's interesting. But let's talk about you. How are you feeling?"

"Oh, *fine*," he said. "And you?"

Laura came out of the bedroom, sat on the sofa beside him. "Cut it out, Richard. Give her a break. Jesus."

He looked at her. "Laura. Know what Laura means in Hebrew?"

"No."

He slowly sat up straight. "Me neither. Think I'll have time to find out? I don't think I'll have time to find out."

"He had to turn up the morphine pump," Laura said. "He was having a lot of pain last night."

I looked at him. He shrugged. "I tried to eat, is why."

"No good, huh?" I said.

"No good. No, I can't eat." He stared into space, seeing something. "I can't eat anymore." He sat unmoving then, lost to his own thoughts. Half a minute passed, maybe more.

Finally, "Could I take a look at your dressing?" I asked.

Laura took his arm, pulled him up. "Come on, Richard."

He shook her off. "I can do it, goddamnit. I'm going." He turned toward me. "Come on, sweet refuge. Save me."

He lay down on the bed, and I started loosening the tape around the edges of his dressing. "I wanted some ribs," he said.

"Pardon?" My voice was muffled, coming from behind the mask I wore.

"I wanted some barbecued ribs, you know, all overdone and smoky and falling off the bone. I ate about half of one, and oh, man . . ."

I cleaned off the insertion site. No drainage, no redness, no swelling.

"I threw it all up, goddamnit. And then I got this pain. Jesus!" He looked at me. "I can have as much morphine as I want, right?"

I nodded. "We'll keep you comfortable, Richard."

"You promise, right?"

"I promise." Here was what I'd been waiting for. An opening. A chance to provide some real comfort. I finished taping his new dressing on.

"You know what, Abby?"

His eyes were so weary. I lay my hand on his shoulder, pulled off my mask. "What?" I asked softly. I could stay for a long time. He was my last appointment for the day. I sat on the bed beside him.

"You can't promise shit."

I sat still.

"You don't know what the fuck you're talking about."

I swallowed, stood up. "I'll do my best to keep you comfortable, Richard."

"That's better," he said. "Now say, 'But I have no idea how all this is going to go down.' "

I said nothing. He raised his eyebrows at me. "Done for the day?"

"Is there anything else you'd like me to do?"

"Yeah. Leave."

I left.

When I arrived at Ida's, I rang the doorbell and heard a faint "Come in." I opened the door but ran into something that prevented its opening fully.

"Ida?" I called. "The door's blocked."

"Oh! Just a minute."

I stood on the front porch, waiting. I heard a screen door bang, and saw that the woman who lived next door had come out to survey me, moving her head from side to side in short, reptilian jerks. She was a thin black woman with wiry white hair, wearing a housecoat and fuzzy slippers and huge glasses on a beaded chain. Her hands were on her hips and she was scowling furiously. "You that nurse?"

"Yes. I'm Abby."

"*I* know."

I smiled at her and for a moment she stopped scowling. But then her face grew fierce again and she pointed her finger at me. "I'm 'on tell you something. You lucky to be alive!"

"Well. . . . Yes."

"Das what I said!"

"And how are you today, Mrs. Johnson?"

"Don't be fooling with me, now."

"I'm not."

"All right, then." She closed her door at the same time that Ida opened hers. "Frankie's got an engine in here," she said. "He's going to fix it up and the guy's going to pay him a lot of money for it, and then we're going out for a steak dinner."

I stepped past a greasy engine laid out on newspaper.

Frankie, sitting at the table with his coffee cup of what was probably whiskey, said, "And what else?"

"Baked potato."

"And . . . ?"

"Cheesecake!" she said, and then looked quickly over at me. "I can cheat sometimes. Sometimes I can just cheat."

I said nothing. What the hell, I was thinking. We're all lucky to be alive.

Toward the end of the week, Richard was watching an old black-and-white movie when I arrived. A man and a woman, both wearing huge shoulder pads, were standing in an office pretending to talk business, but mostly making eyes at each other. Richard nodded at me in a way that was almost friendly. "How are you?" I asked, and then instantly regretted saying something he'd surely use against me.

But he only stood up and said, "A little better, actually. I've been able to get around the apartment pretty good today."

He headed for the bedroom and passed Laura, coming out. She was adjusting a brightly colored scarf around her neck. "Gotta go to work," she said. "But could I talk to you for just a minute first?"

We went into the kitchen and Laura said, in a whisper, "I think he's losing it."

"What do you mean?"

"I think he's getting . . . I don't know, confused. He talks about food all the time. He says that's the worst thing, that he can't eat. He never cared about eating before. But now he stares at food commercials on television like he's seeing a ghost. He's just . . . mesmerized by them. And then he wants me to eat *for* him. Like he'll see something on TV and I'll have to go and get it. Then I have to sit down and eat it in front of him, and he keeps saying, "What's it feel like? How does it taste?" She laughed a little, embarrassed.

"Well," I said, "are you . . . uncomfortable doing that for him?"

She stared at me for a long moment. Then she said, "I do anything Richard asks me to. It's not eating in front of him that bothers me. It's just . . . I'm worried about his mind. I mean, is he going to go crazy before he dies?"

"I don't think so," I said. "I don't know. But I don't think so. There's no reason for him to."

She looked at me.

"I mean physiologically."

"Right," she said.

I put Richard's new dressing on, checked on his equipment, and prepared to leave. "Wait," he said when I picked up my bag.

"Yes?"

"Have you got a minute?"

I hesitated, then put down my bag. "Sure."

He sighed, looked away from me, out the window. "I wanted to tell you that I'm sorry about the way I was to you. I'm not like that, really."

"I know, Richard."

He nodded, looked down, and when he looked up again, I saw tears in his eyes. "I was thinking today about what's going to happen to me after I. . . . You know. I was thinking about being in the ground."

"Uh-huh." I felt something like fear come into me, sit down in my stomach.

"It's just so *weird*, you know. That you won't *be*."

"Yes."

He wiped his eyes. "Well, I just wanted to tell you that it's not you I'm mad at."

"I know that."

"You'll be here tomorrow, right?"

"Eleven o'clock."

"Okay." He nodded. "Okay."

He walked me to the door, shut it softly behind me. I heard the stereo come on as I walked down the steps. Billie Holiday. "Rocky Mountain Blues."

He began wanting me to stay for at least an hour a day. I told my agency that I wanted to have just him as a patient, and they gave Ida to another nurse and took me off the available list for the moment. I didn't tell my husband—he would complain about the income we'd lose. I'd deal with that later if I had to. Perhaps I'd never have to tell him at all.

I sat with Richard in the kitchen, or on the sofa beside him, or most often, because of his weakness, at the foot of his bed. Once, he asked me if I was happy in my marriage. I hesitated, then said, "Well, it's not always easy."

"You know what they say about women who look down when they talk about their marriage, don't you?"

I looked up.

"You know what's funny, Abby? I think you're the one who needs refuge. Do you have a lover?"

"No."

"You've never cheated on your husband?"

"*No!*"

"Ah. So you've thought about it."

I said nothing.

He shook his head. "Too bad."

"What about you, Richard? Do you think you had a perfect relationship?"

"You mean, *have?*"

I flushed, looked down again.

One day, talking about Laura, he said, "We do have a good thing. But I never tell her, 'I love you.' She always wants me to say it, but I don't. He picked up her hairbrush, stroked the back of it. "I've never told that to any woman."

"It's not too late, you know," I said.

He snorted.

"No," I said. "It's not."

He picked up his guitar, strummed it, then handed it to me. "You know how to play one of these?"

I nodded. "I used to love folk songs, I played all the time in college."

"Do one for me."

"Oh, God. I don't know if I remember."

"You will."

He was right. The music came back to me. I sang him a couple of songs: "Great Silkie," "Maid of Constant Sorrow."

"My God," he said. "You have a beautiful voice."

I smiled, embarrassed.

"I mean it. I wish, when it was time, you'd sing to me."

"Oh, well . . ."

"What's the matter? Too tall an order?"

I shrugged. "No, it's . . . I don't know. What are you asking me, Richard?"

"I'm asking you to be here when I die."

I said nothing.

"Can I call you?" He laughed. "I mean, can I have Laura call you?"

I saw the scene. Four-thirty A.M. The phone would ring. I would speak very quietly. Then I would get up, get dressed, drive over to stand beside Laura.

"Yes," I said. "I'll come."

"Okay." He leaned back, smiled. "Aw, don't worry about it. I won't really tell her to call you. What good would *you* do?"

Sometimes he still did things like that.

On Sunday, Laura opened the door in a towel. "Excuse me," she said, and vanished into the bathroom. Richard was lying naked in the bed, calm and satisfied looking. I couldn't believe that the reason for it was what seemed to be the obvious, but it apparently was. But there was something else, too. I could feel him holding it in, waiting to tell me.

I looked at him, raised my eyebrows. "Well?"

"I feel so much better."

I looked toward the bathroom, where I could hear Laura humming. "Good."

"It's not that," he said. "That was nice, but it's something else. I feel really good!"

I waited.

"I mean, nothing hurts. I think I feel like I used to."

I cast about for what to say. I had no idea why this was happening, what it meant. Finally, I said, "That's wonderful, Richard."

"Do you think this means something?"

"What do you mean?"

He sighed, impatient. "Does it *mean* something? Could I be getting better?" He chewed at his lip, his face full of hope.

"You mean, like, something reversing?"

"Yeah."

I looked at him for a long moment. I heard the ticking of his bedside clock. It was heart shaped, pink, covered with rhinestones. A joke, of course. And yet it lived beside his bed.

"I don't know, Richard," I finally said.

He leaned back. "I'm going to a Red Sox game this afternoon. I swear to God, I really am. Laura got us tickets. I'm going to sit out there in the bleachers with everybody else." I saw him there, and then I saw an airplane passing over the stadium, all the passengers looking down and assuming that in the mass of humanity below them, everyone was fine. Everyone was only sitting in the sunshine, watching the ball game.

The next morning, I went out early for groceries. When I got home, the message light was blinking. It was Laura, her voice cold. "I think this is it. I wonder if you could come over as soon as you get this."

I took off my coat, sat at my desk, and called her. When she answered, I said, "What's going on?"

"He's dying."

"How do you know?"

She laughed.

"Did you call the doctor?"

"Yeah."

"And?"

"She came over. Richard was in a whole lot of pain. It started after we got home from the ball game. He did okay while we were there—he even ate a hot dog. But when we got home, all hell broke loose. He cranked up that pump and it didn't help at all. So we called his doctor and she came over and gave him something else. He asked her to get it over with, to give him enough to kill him. She said she couldn't do that, but that she could give him something that would put him to sleep, and he probably wouldn't wake up. He took those pills, and he told me good-bye, but then he woke up again. And you know what he said? He said, "How come I'm not dead?" She sighed, and in it I heard her ironic smile. "I guess it wasn't enough." I heard Richard's voice in the background, and Laura said, "The doctor had to leave—she said she'd put Richard in the hospital, but he wouldn't go. I'm scared. Can you come?"

He was in the bedroom. The shades were pulled, the lamp lit. He was feverish, his lips dried and cracked. As soon as I came into the room, Laura left. "I'll be back," she said, but I wondered.

I sat at the edge of the bed. "Hey."

He shrugged. "What the hell. I think I'm going to go to sleep for this. I've got some more pills. Maybe these will do it."

I nodded. My throat ached.

"I did it."

"What?"

"I told her. Laura."

"Good."

"Abby. I want to ask you something."

"Go ahead."

"Would you . . . I'd like you to take your hair down."

I smiled. "Why?"

"I'd just like to see you with your hair down. I've had some thoughts. About you."

"I know."

"So . . . would you?"

I looked into his eyes. He reached out toward the clip that held my hair up and his hand brushed against my breast. I stood up, startled, then stepped back.

He looked away, embarrassed.

"I'm sorry, I—"

He held up his hand to stop me. "How long will this take? I'm so hot. It hurts so goddamn much. If I take some more of those sleeping pills, if I take what's left, will I wake up?"

"I don't think so."

He nodded, his face calm and unlined. "I will, then. Go and get Laura, will you?"

Laura sat beside him until he fell asleep, then joined me in the living room. "I'm supposed to call the coroner, after," she said.

"Yes."

"Thank you for coming."

"You're welcome."

"And for . . . Thank you."

I nodded, squeezed her hand.

She went back into the bedroom, and the next time she came out, she said simply, "He's gone." She sat down, her back straight, her knees together, her hands folded on her lap. "God, bodies get cold so fast." Her eyes were clear and dry. As were mine. We weren't either one of us going to cry. No. I waited with her for the coroner, and then I went home. I made dinner, and when I sat with my family at the table to eat, how I tasted every bite! In my mind, I told Richard about it, the sweet-sour taste of the sauce on the meat loaf, the buttery smoothness of the potatoes, the nutty green taste of the beans. And the pie. A symphony of apples and cinnamon.

I wanted a break after Richard died. I used some frequent-flyer miles and made arrangements for a weekend visit to a girlfriend who lived in New York City. I'd have some fun, forget about things. Richard's death was a tragedy but these things happened. You move on, and that is all.

My seat mate was an older man, going to visit his grandchildren. He asked me what I did for a living and when I told him, he said he'd just spent a long time taking care of his dying wife. He nearly glowed, talking about her. He said, "It's odd, I know, but caring for her like that? In some ways, it was the best time we ever had. We were really *with* each other. And I can say this honestly: I did everything she asked me to, and even some things she didn't ask me to do but that I could tell she wanted. It brings me peace, that I can say that. I'm sure you know what I mean."

"Yes," I said, "I do know." And I told him that I'd cared for many dying people, and that I found it deeply rewarding, even joyful. Yes.

I ate the snack, read some from the book I'd brought along. My seat mate fell asleep. His mouth was open slightly, and I saw his fists slowly unclench. His magazine slid to the floor, and I leaned over to pick it up. I saw that he'd been reading an article about whales, about their mournful, singing sounds. I thought about them, deep in the ocean below me. I looked out the window, but I couldn't see the ocean, or anything else. There was only blackness, my face looking back at itself. And then, as though it were a tangible thing I could hold in my hands, I saw my regret at not doing everything Richard asked me to do. I put myself back in our last day together, in that moment of refusal. But this time:

I put down my bag, step out of my shoes. I let down my hair, feel it fall soft and fragrant onto my shoulders. I unzip my jeans, slide them off, pull my sweater over my head. I remove my underwear. Then I lie down beside him. I feel the heat of his fever before I touch his skin. I know his pain, and so I move him very gently toward me. I sing softly to him, stroke his temple, ease it all, ease it, until it is over.

I envisioned this, and I realized that love comes in all forms, and is always about more than we can know. I saw that there are exquisite acts of tenderness lying latent in all of us, waiting only for our permission to come into being. I put the magazine into the seat pocket of the man beside me, and I turned to look into his sleeping face. Then I made a movement in the air between us. I started with my hands together, pulled them apart, and down, and then slowly back together. I saw that I had made a circle. A whole other world in which to do things right.

Take This Quiz

After she is sure the children are asleep, Ursula joins her husband in the family room. Jack is watching *MotorWeek* and absentmindedly eating potato chips. He is somewhat overweight: his shirt gaps between the bottom buttons. When Ursula comes into the room, he pats the sofa cushion beside him, gestures toward the television. "They're showing how to clean out clogged fuel injectors."

Ursula sighs, a small sound, and sits down beside him. "Does anyone know you watch this?"

He shrugs. "Who cares?"

She closes the chip bag, puts it aside. "Jack? Could we turn this off?"

He turns toward her. "What's the matter?"

"Nothing. I just want to talk to you."

"Is something wrong?"

"No."

"Okay," he says, his gaze returning to the screen. "Just let me see them review the new Chrysler. Then we can talk."

Ursula rolls her eyes, gets up to go and sort the laundry. When she met Jack in college and learned he was a physics major, she imagined long, complex, romantic discussions wherein Jack would explain the workings of the universe to her. Now, fifteen years later, he is a motorhead who views intimate conversation as being roughly equivalent to hernia repair. She kicks at the pile of under-wear, separates it from the towels.

When she returns to the family room, the television set is off. She finds this encouraging. She sits on the sofa next to Jack, draws her feet up under her. Jack kisses her neck, runs his hand across her breasts.

"Don't," she says, pulling away. His easy passion infuriates her. He doesn't know how to work up to things properly. You don't just leap *into* things, she has tried to tell him. You *think* about what you're doing before you do it. Then things have more *meaning*. But Jack goes for the easy, the superficial. She regrets this for him, despairs of him ever learning what life offers when you dig down deep. He really should make an effort to know himself, she thinks. She pulls a magazine off the coffee table. "There's a quiz in here I'd like you to take with me."

"A quiz? About what?"

"About whether you're happy or not. I'd really like us to take it together." She opens the magazine to a dog-eared page. "ARE YOU *REALLY* HAPPY?" is written in large, boldfaced print at the top of the page. Then, in smaller print, "*Answer these ten questions and learn the truth!*"

"What's going on, Ursula?" Jack says. "Do you have something you want to tell me?"

"No!" she says. "I just wanted us to take a little quiz together. It might be interesting. It might *show* us something." She crosses her arms petulantly. "I've watched *Gus's Garage* with *you*!"

"Fine," he sighs.

She tosses her hair back, wets her lips, and reads aloud. "Number one. 'Does your romantic partner satisfy your needs?' "

From down the hall, they hear a faint "Can I have a drink of water?"

Jack jumps up. "I'll go."

"Wait a minute," she says. "Sometimes he says that in his sleep." But in a few moments, they hear, "I want a *driiiinnnnk!*"

"There's something wrong with him," Ursula says. "All he does is drink water. I *gave* him a drink right before he went to bed. I'm going to get him tested!"

"Relax," Jack says. "I'll go."

Ursula sits glumly on the sofa until Jack returns. When he sits down, he says, "You know, it's been a long time since we had a nice dinner together. This weekend, let's go somewhere. Do you think Ruthie can sit?"

"Jack," she says.

"Yeah?"

"We are taking a quiz."

"I know," he says.

"So why are you talking about this weekend? What is your chronic resistance to finding *out* about yourself?"

"First of all," he says, "I don't have a *chronic resistance* to anything. Secondly, if I did, a *magazine* quiz would not be my preferred method for illumination."

"I think this could help you, Jack. If nothing else, it's something you could do for *me*. I'd appreciate it."

He is quiet for a moment. Then, "All right, Ursula. We'll take the damn quiz."

"Number one," she says again.

"I remember the question," Jack says.

"Well?"

"Well what?"

"You go first," she says happily.

Jack takes the magazine from her, looks at the cover. It features an openmouthed model with a deliriously vacant look on her face. Blurbs for the stories inside surround her. "Where'd you get this, anyway?" he asks.

"At the *grocery* store."

Jack stares critically at the magazine, his lips shaped as though he is smelling something bad. Then he hands it back to her. "So what's *your* answer?"

"What do you care?" she asks.

Jack snaps on the television. Ursula takes the remote control and snaps it off.

"My answer is yes!" she says.

"Fine," he says. "So is mine. More or less."

"What's *that* supposed to mean?"

"Nothing."

"Well, there are no qualifiers allowed. 'Does your romantic partner satisfy your needs?' Is your answer yes, or no?"

"It's yes, Ursula. Okay? It's yes." He rubs the back of his neck, looks away from her.

"Good," she says. She is heartened by his discomfort. Now they're getting somewhere. "Number two," she says. " 'How often do you fantasize about living another life altogether?' "

"A lot," Jack says.

Ursula looks at him. "You do? . . . Why?"

"I don't know. I just think about other kinds of lives, that's all."

She sniffs. "Like with your twelve-year-old secretary, I suppose."

"No," he sighs. "Not with my secretary. Did it ever occur to you that maybe I fantasize about being a trapeze artist?"

She looks at him for a long moment. Then she says, "No, you don't."

"Well, I do think about other kinds of lives," he says. "Ones I've missed. I mean, I really wanted to be a doctor. Did you know that? I had a medical kit when I was a kid, went around the neighborhood bandaging things, even broken limbs on trees. It was . . . magical, thinking I could help heal. But I never took the MCAT, never bothered pursuing it. I don't know why. And sometimes now I think, Wow, it's really too late. I'm never going to get to be a doctor."

"Well, *I* don't fantasize much about another life," she says. "I don't know why *you* do. What do you suppose that means, that you do?"

"Look. You're the one who wanted to take this stupid quiz. If all you're going to do is get aggravated, let's forget it."

"I'm not *aggravated*. I *like* doing this. It's interesting. And it's good, you know, to do a little self-analysis. You can't be afraid of a little discomfort, Jack! That's what makes you change, makes you grow. It's how you find things *out*! I mean, look: I'm finding out that I'm pretty happy. I didn't really *know*." She rearranges herself, reads, "Three. 'Are you more than ten pounds overweight?' "

"Now, what the hell is *that* in there for?" Jack asks.

"It happens to be very important what you weigh," Ursula says. "Overweight people are not happy."

"Bullshit," Jack says.

Ursula sits up straighter, turns to Jack. "You may pretend not to worry about it—"

"I *don't* worry about it!"

"You may *pretend* not to worry about it," Ursula says, "but it does affect your self-image."

"*I'll* tell you what affects my self-image! Sitting around taking some ridiculous *mag*azine quiz that purports to tell me whether or not I'm *happy!* You think *MotorWeek* is stupid? Next to this, it's Feynman's lectures on quantum electrodynamics!"

"Maybe," Ursula says quietly, "this quiz is just bringing up some things you need to think about, Jack. Maybe it's time to stop working so hard at keeping your blinders on. You deny *everything.* Your life is a lie. You need to *see* things!"

"Why," he asks, "when you see them for both of us? Why don't you just go right on telling me how I *really* feel, what I'm *missing,* Ursula? You're so good at it. You seem to enjoy it so much. I'd hate to deny you." He leaves the room. She hears him going down to the basement.

Ursula straightens up the family room, finds a fire truck and several Legos stuck behind a chair cushion. She feels an odd numbness as she picks them up; it's as though her fingers aren't quite touching the toys, as though some invisible lining is between them and her. She carries the toys into the boys' room, then goes to stand beside their bunk beds. She straightens their covers, inspects them in the dim light. They are so beautiful. No matter how exasperated she has gotten with them during the day, when she sees them sleeping at night she aches with love for them. Jack is right, she thinks. They have a good life. Why does she analyze, question so much? They are lucky. They *are* happy! She will go downstairs to get him. They'll watch *Nightline* together. She'll make some dip for the chips. Maybe she'll wear something special to bed. The red nightgown with the slit cut up high. Not that Jack ever needs incentive.

She goes into the basement. Jack is at his workbench, sanding the edges of a toy box he is making for the boys. He looks up when Ursula comes in, then away.

"I'm sorry I made you take that quiz," she says. "I just . . . Sometimes I wish we could feel things more alike. It could make us closer, you know? I thought if we talked about whether or not we were really happy—"

He stops sanding. "I'll tell you something, Ursula. I never saw much point in asking yourself if you're happy, never saw the reason for that obsessive kind of self-inventory. It bores me. I'm a simple guy, Ursula. I love you and the kids, I like cars. I don't ask for a lot more than for us all to be together and healthy. That makes me happy. I'm sorry I can't be a malcontent for you. What do you want me to do? Tell you all my regrets, my failures?" He looks at her, takes in a deep breath. "I hate my job, Ursula. I'm sick to death of always being the one to initiate sex. You turned out . . . sillier than I expected. I believe nuclear war is inevitable, that existence is inherently pointless, that it's too late to save the environment. Is that what you want to hear? Is that the kind of romantic prelude you long for?" He puts down his sandpaper. "I'm going to bed."

He squeezes past her out the door, treads heavily up the stairs. Ursula stands before the toy box for a moment, then turns out the light and heads upstairs herself. She is aware of a sudden and profound fatigue.

After she is ready for bed, she climbs in beside Jack, nestles up to him. She is wearing perfume, the red nightgown. She moves closer, whispers, "Are you awake?" She hears his breath go evenly in and out. The familiarity of it calms her. "Jack?" She moves her hand across his stomach.

"I don't want to talk anymore, okay?" He takes her arm from around him, moves away from her. A first.

"Okay." She lies still, her eyes open, thinking. She is remembering the time she was nine and took apart a jewelry box she loved, to see what made the ballerina turn around. Though she paid careful attention to each step, when she tried to reassemble it, it didn't work the way it had before. No one else could fix it, either. The ballerina stayed in place, permanently turned away, oblivious to the music she had danced to before.

Martin's Letter to Nan

Dear Nan,

I feel like a fool, writing this. Not knowing if I'll ever give it to you. Wondering what the hell I can say on a page that I can't say to you in person when you get back. But reading your letters has made me think that maybe there's something to this writing thing. Maybe it's easier to say certain things when you're alone and thinking about a person, rather than being with her. At any rate, I'll give it a try. I've got your pile of letters here beside me, I've got a cigar and a glass of scotch. Here goes.

First of all, I am angry. Not as much as I was when I first found your note, but I am still angry. How would you have felt if you'd gotten out of bed, come downstairs, and found some note saying I was leaving and I didn't know when I'd be coming back? You'd have been furious, Nan, admit it. You'd have been on the phone to your damn girlfriends, telling them not only that I had left, but other things you're pissed off about as well. These would be things you would never dream of telling me—oh yes, I know you do that, because I've overheard you. You usually start with, "He is *driving* me *crazy,"* and then you reveal something very personal about me. I want to say right now that at least I never do that to you, Nan. I don't go running off with my male friends and say terrible things about you. You remember that week or so when you were having trouble with gas? We didn't know what it was, but Jesus Christ, you were farting to beat the band. We were going to take you to the doctor and then it all of a sudden stopped. You think I ever told the guys about that? But you talk about me to your women friends all the time, carry on about things I can't help any more than you could help farting. My *level of cleanliness.* My *denseness.* I don't see the flower the way you see the flower, okay, Nan? I'm *wired* differently. Most men are. And the ones that aren't, I don't think you'd be much interested in.

I wonder sometimes why men and women persist in living together, especially after the kids are gone. You can understand the biology of it, the need for us to be together to have and raise children. But after that, isn't it just a trial? The way we're constantly accommodating each other? The way, for example, I never get to smoke my cigars in the house unless you're off on some trip to "save" yourself. The way I feel I must ask permission to put on a CD that *I* like. Why don't people just organize same-sex colonies? I wonder. Visit each other if you girls can tear yourselves away from talk, talk, talking and if we can leave the ball games. Think of it, a group of people all living together who share the same opinion about what should be done with the toilet seat. About whether or not you should put on some tight-ass outfit and drive into the city to see the opera—hmmm, now there's a hard one. About whether it will cut your life expectancy in half if you eat a piece of beef jerky. About whether a bed must be made every morning, the wet towels removed immediately from the floor, the whites done with the whites, the newspaper thrown away the second we're done reading it—or before! Why *don't* we separate—keep each other in our wills, attend graduations and weddings and funerals together, date, even, but live apart? I don't know, I guess it's because love works that way, that the person who bedevils you is also the one you need.

Well, I have read what I've written so far and it's a bunch of crap. But you know what? I don't care. I do not care. That's what a good dose of a good scotch will do for you.

So let's just see. Let's just see what you wrote and let's see what I have to say back. But first, my dear, another drink. Cheers.

In your first letter, you mention Kotex. Now, what in the hell am I meant to do with information like that, Nan? And you say you sat at the breakfast table with me, acting like nothing was wrong, when there was a hurricane inside you. What I want to know is, why didn't you say anything? I sensed what I thought was a kind of restlessness in you, but I let it go. You are often restless, darling. You are often a pain in the ass. I let it go because of the times when you are not.

But you might have said something. In a way that would let me know what was *really* going on. For example, when you were hurting at the thought of our daughter being gone after she graduated, how hard would it have been to say to me, "Will you miss Ruthie?" I might have told you something.

Well. I write that and then I sit back and read it and think, if truth be told, I probably would not have said much. I probably would have shrugged. I probably *would* have said, "Well, she'll visit." And so what? It is not my job or obligation to process things the way you do, Nan. But it is your obligation to try to tell me why things are a problem for you so you're not always walking around with this dreamy, tragic look on your face. So that you're not waking up and clutching at rocks you keep in your bedside table drawer, for Christ's sake. There you are, a married woman, lying beside her husband in their bed at night, turning to *rocks* for comfort! Should you not accept *some* of the blame for that?

Now in the second letter you tell me about a dream you had. The truth is, and I say this in the kindest of ways, Nan, I am just not interested in dreams—yours or anyone's. They don't matter to me, they matter only to the person who had them. And every time you tell me your dreams, you stand hawklike before me, watching to see if I'll "get it." And I don't *want* to get it. I don't want to *hear* it. If I said urgently to you, "I had this *dream* last night," would *you* be so interested? Maybe you would. But only so that you could take it apart and psychoanalyze me some more. Or so that you could see where *you* figure in, in my dream. You are like a kid that way, Nan, always needing so much to be in the center of everything. More than other women I've known. And I have known my share. You don't know about all of them. You think you do, but you don't. Some things weren't worth telling you. Some things were too hard to tell you. I loved a girl when I was fifteen and she was fourteen, and she died of leukemia. That, for example. Which I still don't want to talk about, but there, you never knew that, did you? Or the time I went to my thirtieth high school reunion and you didn't want to come and Sandy Miller offered to

Well, suffice it to say you don't know everything. You are not the only one who runs deep, Nan, who does not say everything because of the feeling that you will not be understood.

I know I'm being tough on you, okay? It is my right and my privilege. It is what you owe me, the opportunity to state my piece. You felt you had the right to leave. I now have the right to respond to your leaving. I hope you will read this all the way through. Please read this all the way through. I don't know where I'm going, but I know I'm not through yet. I am warming to this.

Ah yes, now we come to the side roads portion of your correspondence. Your old complaint of how I never want to take the side roads. How many times will I have to tell you this? The side roads take five times as long, and you expect me to *get* you places. You sit beside me looking out the window, making up your little fantasies about everything you see, wanting to stop at every peach stand and every antique store, and I'm the one who has to drive, drive, drive. And I know what you're going to say. You're going to say you *offer* to drive and I hardly ever *let* you. Right. Because if you drive you get on your beloved side roads and you get behind a tractor and then you're afraid to pass. So there we are, off to a place five hundred miles away and driving eighteen miles per hour. It makes me feel like I could tear off the roof of my car with my teeth and eat it. If we go on a trip, it's to *get* somewhere. The side roads are all right for a mile or so but then you've got to get going or you'll never *get* there. Easy for you to be the romantic artiste, the sighing sufferer, when you know that good old Martin will be taking care of the practical things, such as getting you where you need to be when you need to be there. And Martin will lock the doors at night and turn off all the lights you left on and if the dog starts puking at 4 A.M., it'll be Martin who gets up to let him out. A noise downstairs that wakes you up? Why, just send Martin down to take the bullet. *Then* call the cops.

I'll say one thing about your letter about the bed-and-breakfast—at least you sounded cheerful there. At least you got off yourself and onto something else. You've been so self-obsessed lately, Nan, worrying about how you're getting older and losing your looks—oh, don't worry, you don't have to say a word to me, I know all about it. I know too that you're worrying about the wrong things. Instead of your thighs, worry about the fact that you've lost your sense of sexual self-assurance—to put it plainly, Nan, you're no fun in bed anymore. Trying to cover things up. Not wanting the light on. No interest in trying anything new, or doing any of the wilder things we used to do with some frequency. When will you women understand that what turns men on isn't what you think? Sure, I look at the beautiful girls who walk past our tables when we're having dinner out. But not as much as you do, Nan! And don't you know that I'd take a lusty, happy, overweight fifty-year-old woman over one of those skinny, miserable, navel-gazing twenty-year-olds anytime? I don't know if all men are like this but I think most of them are: what we want is someone who likes herself, who finds herself attractive. It gives us ideas. Makes us think maybe we ought to like her and find her attractive, too. A woman who knows how to find the music, Nan, that's what we like. You don't seem to find the music anymore. You seem to spend your days standing at the window. At least that's what you were doing before you left. Maybe you're better now.

I wonder if

Phone just rang. Marion Kirshner. You know, the divorcée who moved in a few doors down a couple of months ago. Always out in her garden half naked. She was wondering if you're home yet—she'd heard from our neighbors that you were on vacation, that's what I told them. Nope, I said, she's not home yet. Well, she said, how about dinner tonight? I said fine. I said we'll go on over to Roger's and have him burn us a couple of steaks and we'll knock back a couple of martinis. Do I say this to make you jealous? Why, yes, I do, Nan. I don't have any intention of doing anything but dinner. No interest, to tell you the truth. For one thing, that woman puts on makeup with a trowel. But you should know that on the open market, I wouldn't last long. And what better thing to drink a toast to, won't you excuse me.

Finished the bottle with that one. Hadn't realized we were so short. Guess you've been the one to keep us supplied in liquor, too. Yesterday I ran out of toilet paper at a most inconvenient moment. Looked in the drawer for the extra roll and *nada*. Shit! I said. And then had to laugh, of course. Sat there awhile and thought about the fact that it's been nice to have things *there*. That I may fix everything that breaks, including things that you should know how to do, it's just obvious, for Christ's sake, but you do keep the house well supplied. There is not a goddamn thing to eat here now.

Well, you say in this next letter that you passed a field and the cows standing there looked like chess pieces. I would have liked hearing that if I'd been with you, Nan. As I too like the taste of so many things we've eaten together, but I never say so because you always get there first. Oh, Martin! you say. Taste this! *Taste* it! Isn't it *good*? And you're so insistent, Nan, that the joy leaves for me. You make me feel contrary. You make me want to say, NO, okay? *No*, it is *not* so good. No, I do *not* taste it. I know, I know, I can hear you saying how hostile I am, how HOSTILE MEN ARE. You women say that all the time, and you're always making fun of men. Just how do you think you'd react if men did that to you? If a man put a sticker on his bumper saying *A man without a woman is like a fish without a bicycle*, some woman lawyer would come along and sue him. Oh yes, Nan, when you're on your little road trip I hope you give that one some thought, about how men have taken just as much bullshit as women have. If not more!

But anyway, the point I was trying to make about the tasting thing is I wish you would just let me have a chance to say something first. Let me be the one to say it first. Oh, Martin, look at that painting! Look at it! Oh Martin, listen to the violin, *listen* to it. It's like you're a culture Nazi. I see it, Nan, I hear it, I taste it, I fucking smell it, I just do not need to TALK TALK TALK TALK TALK about it!

Well, I'm sorry. But I needed to make that point. If you'd just let me go first, once in a while. Or if you could just stand quietly beside me, trusting that I do see things, if only in my own way. And what is wrong with that?

I'll tell you something, Nan. Sometimes I want to say something to you about myself but I just don't. Sometimes it's because *you're* usually talking, but sometimes it's—well, I don't know what. Maybe shyness. Maybe I'm ashamed that if I tell you, you'll think I'm weak. But I had dreams just like you as a child. I had plans and adventures that were interesting, too. *Like what, Martin?* I can hear you saying. Well, like this.

When I was eight, there was some newspaper article speculating about where the winter Olympics would be held. And I thought—I don't know why, but I thought, well, how about I invite them to use my backyard? The idea just grew and grew. I thought about it every night before bed. I wanted all the details to be worked out before I wrote to the Olympics committee and offered my place. I figured I'd ask the neighbors to pull their cars into their driveways so as to leave room on the street for parking. The ski jump could be off the garage roof. I worried about there being enough snow, so I was going to also ask the neighbors if I could shovel their walks and driveways and then use their snow. I saw a picture of the queen of England on the front page of the paper and I thought maybe she might like to come, and I was going to invite her to have dinner with the family. But I wanted to make sure the little kids ate in the other room—no spilled milk or nose picking in front of Her Majesty. Every night I lay in my bed and thought about it and got myself so excited I couldn't sleep. And when I was finally ready to send the invitation, it was announced where the Olympics would be held. And it was not my backyard, because I was too late in asking—that was my feeling, that if only I had asked in time. . . . And I went into my bedroom and lay on my bed and punched the pillow over and over. And then I went out to throw the baseball against the side of house, because things do not last with me like they do with you. You don't get over things quickly, as I do. I wish you would, as long as we are being so honest here. I wish you would not hold on to anger the way you do. And also I wish the house would not be so crowded with crap, so that I could *move.* And I wish you would stop buying fat-free EVERYTHING. Eat a real hot dog once in a while, knock yourself out.

Well, now I have read the part about your sleeping in the woods by yourself and I wish you hadn't done that, Nan. It's not safe. It's one thing to take some time to go on a trip and another altogether to sleep alone in the woods when you have no idea where you are. You are not a strong woman, you know. Carrying in one grocery bag at a time. You are not a strong woman. And you don't know how men can be when a woman is alone and vulnerable. It makes them get ideas. Even a good man might think to himself, Well, what the hell? That was stupid and I intend to talk to you more about it when you get home. Remind me.

You say you used to get up and watch Ruthie sleep in her crib when she was a little baby. Well, so did I, Nan. And you know what else? I watched her sleep all her life. When she was seven and she slept with all her stuffed animals all lined up, when she was eleven and slept with her Barbies, when she was fifteen and slept with her diary. The night before she left for college, I watched her sleep for a good fifteen minutes, I swear. Just stood there, the moon so bright it was like sunshine. And then I went outside into the backyard and onto the patio where the swing set I built for her used to be. I sat in a chair and leaned back and looked up into the sky and I thought about her whole life with us, and then damned if I didn't start to cry. I thought about the first time I held her, scared shitless by how light she was, I thought a breeze would lift her right out of my arms. I thought about the time she was three and she got those patent leather shoes she loved so much all full of mud, and I realized I was not going to be able to protect her from everything after all. I thought of her sixth birthday party, how dressed up she got in her favorite pink dress, pink ribbons in her hair, I think you even painted her fingernails pink, and then all the other girls came in jeans. I thought of the time she was fourteen and I came into her room and she didn't see me, and she was standing before her mirror using her hairbrush to be the microphone and lip-synching with Madonna. Her braces were gleaming and she was trying so hard to look sexy and I didn't know whether to laugh or cry. I thought of the time I got up late at night to take a leak and I looked out the window and saw her sitting in some guy's car, kissing him, and I wanted to go out and bust the guy's head in. I didn't tell you any of that, Nan. It didn't seem necessary. The difference between you and me is that I don't need someone to validate every thought I have, and I wish, frankly, that you were more like me that way. The weight of having to affirm everything for you is nearly unbearable sometimes. I have often wished for a mannequin Martin I could sit at the dinner table who would be programmed to say, "Oh, uh-huh," in the properly *engaged* manner every ninety seconds. And I'd take a beer and a burger and extra-fat potato chips down to the basement to watch the Red Sox.

Now, I remember that day when I was leaving for work and you started in with something and yes, I did tell you to have an affair. But it wasn't because I really meant it. It was because I was so tired of trying to please you when there was no pleasing you. "Martin, I need romance," you said, as I was *walking out the door to go to work,* Nan. What was I to do? I had a meeting with thirty-five people in half an hour and I was running late. What was I to do? Call and say, Listen, I need to talk to my wife, she needs romance? Or say, How about you just fly all those people who came in to meet with me back to where they came from, my wife is too lonely? You were in your robe, Nan, the whole day before you. I was in my suit, headed out the door to go to the office. Quit, then! I can imagine you saying. I never wanted this lifestyle! Money means nothing to me! Well, you just think about that one, Nan. Think really hard about that one. If you really don't mind not having a lot of money, yes, I will consider retiring. Don't you think I have my own trials to consider at work? Do you really think *you* have to tell *me* about stuffy conference rooms? Yes, you come home and we'll talk about my retiring. I would like to live in a house such as the one you have described to me, but I'd like a little input too, Nan. Such as I want a pool table and a flat-screen TV the size of North Carolina. And a vending machine, which I told you about once and you just started laughing. But I want a vending machine, I think it would be cool. And hold on to your hat, Nan: I want to smoke my cigars INSIDE. We can figure something out, as long as we're going to be building a new house anyway—we can make the basement extremely well ventilated, whatever, but I want to smoke cigars in there and I want a refrigerator to hold beer and *only* beer. Want an opener built onto the side. I want leather furniture soft as butter and I do not want to see one, not one, *not one* "decorator" pillow or afghan anywhere. Nor any flowers. Nor any artwork beyond the dartboard I'll put up.

Now your letter where you ask me some questions. Have I ever had an affair? No. Have I ever thought of it? Yes. Yes, yes, and yes, how could I not? Once Jocelyn, that assistant I had that you never liked, she showed me a lingerie catalogue and asked me to help her pick out something that her boyfriend would like. I had a boner the side of a Katz's salami, it's a good thing I was behind the desk. But Nan, I made you a promise. I meant it. Who knows if it's a good idea or not, monogamy? But I made the promise and probably it is a good idea whose worth we might not fully understand until later. I can tell you this: I have watched you as you made dinner on summer nights, standing barefoot with your apron on, and I have seen the late afternoon sun light up your hair and I have noticed the care with which you prepare our food and I have loved you so fiercely it hurt, it truly made for a hurt in my chest. And I have thought at times like that if anyone tried to take you from me, I would kill them. And I have been glad that I have stayed faithful to you despite what have been many opportunities. You must know that this happens for men, especially for those who are traveling. I remember two prostitutes at the bar, when Dan Guthridge and I went over to Amsterdam. My God, they were beautiful. We bought them a few drinks, okay? I never told you because you wouldn't have understood. You buy women like that drinks because you want to check out the cleavage, you like the way their dresses ride up when they cross their legs, and you're thinking about the many, many favors they could do for you, yes you are, but I didn't do anything, I came back to the room and there were the T-shirts in my suitcase that you had folded. And it was a bad time for us, Nan, we were not getting along so well, I was not spending my evenings having my ego built up as I had been in the bar. But I was glad anyway that I had not betrayed you. I sat on the bed and I thought about calling you but as I said we weren't getting along so well, so I did not. I jerked off and went to sleep. So no, I have not had an affair. And I say to you again now that I will not.

All right. I did cancel my physical. I don't need any colonoscopy and I know if I have a physical he will say did you ever have that colonoscopy and I will say no and then he'll start telling me all about why I need a colonoscopy and did I quit smoking cigars yet. Then he'll ask me about the Patriots like we're sitting at the bar when meanwhile he has his finger up my butt. Listen, Nan, we part ways here, and I'm becoming more and more convinced that my way is right. You go and get physicals if you want, but I don't want to anymore. Not every year. Every five years or so is enough. If I get diabetes or high blood pressure or some other damn thing, then you can say, See? I told you! and won't that bring you some pleasure. But I canceled my physical and I don't want to hear a word about it.

You have spent some time in your letters talking about men's cruelty to women. I have to say that it works both ways. I know men are stronger, that in abuse cases it's usually the man hurting the woman. But I just want to say that it works both ways. You know Charlie Stevens, right? You know what kind of verbal lashings that guy endures every day? Nothing he does is right. He ruined her. He gives her nothing. He's a nobody who embarrasses her. He's too fat, his hair is too thin. Blah, blah, blah, she never shuts up. And he feels it. That man hasn't stood up straight and looked out from behind his own eyes for years. I don't think he remembers anything about who he used to be.

What I want to say to you, Nan, and I think you'll agree with this, what I want to say is that what's needed is just some mutual respect. That's all. Let me have my ways, try to learn to appreciate my ways, and I'll do the same for you.

I've missed you. Knowing you are not here, I've looked for you. And I've seen you: reading in the living room, drinking coffee at the breakfast table, folding back the bedclothes in your precise preparation for sleep. Did you know that sometimes I wake up at night and listen to the soft sounds of your breathing? What I feel about knowing you are there—there when snow falls, when spring comes, when thunderstorms seem to shake the foundation, when the roses beneath our bedroom window are in full bloom and when they die and when they come back again—could fill a book. Or at least a letter. This one, perhaps.

I want you to come home. I will be glad to see your familiar face, to take your familiar hand, to lie down with you on the bed we picked out together so many years ago. I want to let you talk to someone who wants to listen. I have some things to say, too, and then I hope we can just stay there in the quiet, feeling all that we have together.

Oh, Nan. In honor of every bit of it.

Love,
Martin

What Stays

When I was eight years old, my mother began to leave me and my two sisters alone a lot. She always meant it to be temporary, and she always prepared us for it a few days in advance so we wouldn't be scared. Of course, we were scared anyway. The oldest of us, my sister Helen, felt that the best way to care for us was to ignore us. I don't blame her in retrospect—it was too much to put on a twelve-year-old. But then, I would sit alone in the living room, fearing my mother was gone forever and longing for Helen to read to me, to dress and undress my dolls with me, to suggest that of course my mother would return.

She left us for missions that came along—she would attend funerals of people she deemed heroes by virtue of their obituaries. "She was only twenty-three," she would say sadly, on her way out. Or, "He spent thirty years as a teacher to the blind. Imagine!" If she read about a strike, she would go to walk the picket line. Once she went to meet a woman with whom she'd had a prison correspondence, and that time she was gone for a week.

My father worked for the railroad as a switchman, and he came home tired and silent. My mother disappointed him, but he had given up trying to change her. She was always so friendly with him, acted like he was a welcome guest; but he saw her as another job, one he essentially couldn't do. They passed by each other, my mother smiling, my father sighing. I don't know when they loved each other. It must have been long before I was born, when my father saw my mother as a wild thing he wanted. He didn't count on her not calming down, I suppose. He lived like a shadow in our house, like a suggestion of a person. He spoke so rarely that when he did, we would startle and stare at him.

Sometimes my mother would get interested in things she could do at home. She decided to raise dogs, and she supervised our mongrel bitch from mating through birth. After the puppies arrived, though, she seemed disappointed at the dog's natural competence. She picked the nursing puppies up and examined their tiny mouths for a white stain to make sure they were getting something, and the babies squealed in distress. She neatened the warm little row of their bodies while the bitch regarded her with a baleful stare. She looked in at odd times of the day to be sure the puppies weren't crushing one another when they slept, and they never were. Disheartened, she concentrated on the mother, giving her too-frequent meaty treats, which were listlessly accepted. Then she said there was clearly no point in trying to help nature, and left them all alone. When the puppies were five weeks old, my father brought them to the pound. When my mother found out, she wept.

She thought of baking as an occupation—she made wonderful things—and her idea was to walk the morning streets with warm caramel rolls. She made different varieties and gave them to us for breakfast. "What do you think?" she would say. "Better when they're stickier, or drier? Do they need a cherry on top? Should I use nuts, or not?" When she found a recipe we agreed on, she began mapping out routes. "Fifty cents apiece," she would say. "It could add up." My father finally argued her out of doing it. "For God's sake, Marion," he said. "Please."

This all happened in the fifties, when other mothers stayed home making dinner from cookbooks, wearing calm and sensible clothes with aprons over them. These mothers didn't go anywhere, as far as I could see. They sent their children to school and they were there when their children returned. They gave out snacks, served on a plate, with a napkin beside it. They didn't yell.

My mother would yell—loudly, passionately. Then she would apologize, drag all three of us up to her bedroom and line us up on the bed. "I don't know why I did that," she would say. She would cry and wring her hands and stare at us. Then she would put each of our faces between her hands and kiss us. "Forgive me," she would say. "I love you."

We kids kept one another company, raised ourselves, excused the obvious problems of our mother. We had no outside friends. That didn't seem to matter too much, though. We made allies and enemies of one another in kaleidoscopic ways. We weren't bored.

Then one day when we came home from school, we found my mother stonelike at the kitchen table. She wouldn't talk, or even look at us, for a long time. When she finally did, she said, "Apparently it's time for me to 'take care of myself.' I'm going to see a head doctor. Otherwise, your father will leave me. He told me last night, can you imagine? See a shrink or he will divorce me. You'd think I had something contagious. You'd think I was dangerous." She laughed, a small, shaky sound. I saw her for the first time then as fragile. We were all there with her, and she addressed us as though she were heading a meeting: She had us sit down at the kitchen table and then she stood up and said, "Before I do any- thing, I want to say this: You are children. And right now you are as smart as God. As you get older, something will try to take you from yourself. You'll start stuffing your brain with numbers, with facts you'll need to memorize, and all of it will be something someone else has come up with. You will learn to ignore your own genius, let yourself wither on the vine out of deference to some- one else's opinion. It's a damn shame." She took a sip of coffee from the cup before her, and then held it out toward me. "You want some?" I shook my head no. "You see?" she said. "Smart as God." She went over to lean against the kitchen sink. "I saw deep into your eyes, each of you, right after you were born. What a sight! I swear, you knew everything. You would be calm, looking out into the world as though it were new and familiar all at once. And then, before we were done looking at each other, they would take you away from me, begin doing strange, rough things to you. By the time I got you back, you would have clothes on, and you would be crying, and I would feel so sorry for you. I would rock you, and whisper to you, 'It's all right. I know you.' And you would calm down, lean into me so naturally it felt as though we were both the same thing." She looked at Helen. "Do you remember?"

Helen had stood transfixed before her, as we all had. Now she took her glasses off and wiped at her eyes with the heel of her hand. Then she stood straighter and said, "No. I don't remember. I don't remember anything. How could I? I was just a baby, Ma. You don't remember from when you were a baby."

I wanted to rush to my mother, hug her around the waist, and say that I did remember. For although I couldn't remember any- thing that she said specifically, her words sounded true to me, reached out and connected deeply to a place somewhere between my heart and my stomach. I believed her. I could feel her rightness. And I ached for her brave admission, lying seemingly unaccepted before us all.

She put her cup in the sink and turned away from us for a minute. I was afraid she was crying, but she wasn't. When she turned back, she said, "I love each of you, with all my heart. I never saw any reason not to have you, and I'd have more, but your father . . . Well, I want to tell you that I know I'm different. I suppose it's just all too much for you. But here, listen: when you see something everyone else takes for granted, just think about whether or not it's really true, or necessary." She paused, looked out the window, and then back at us. "Look, houses are square boxes, right?" We nodded. "They don't need to be," she said. "Think of what else we could do! Why, people don't even need to separate themselves so! We could have had other plans, other ways to live, but people don't trust themselves. One gets an idea, the others follow. People are uncomfortable with something different. But it doesn't mean it's wrong. You need to know that. You really do." And then she did begin to cry, and we stood awkwardly around her, until finally I went over and began to pat her back. My hand seemed much too small against her to help at all. She covered her face with her hands and wept, with loud, laughlike sounds. One by one, silently, we left her there.

She began seeing a doctor on Tuesdays. She would put on a suit and some high heels that we used to play with. She came home with a spiral notebook full of her own observations—she apparently took notes as violently as the doctor did. And then, abruptly, she stopped going. She said that the doctor never laughed, that his stance was too tight, that the photos of his children in his office were all covered with dust, that he had more problems than she ever dreamed of.

Then there came a morning when she wouldn't get up, when she lay motionless in bed, staring at nothing. I stood by the door, thinking that if I said the right thing, she would smile, then laugh, then hold me against her and say, "Oh, you know, don't you?" I sat on the bed once, lowered myself carefully next to her, tried to look into her eyes. She stared straight ahead. Her breathing was so quiet. She was like an alive dead person. She scared me, and I ran to Helen. "She's sick," Helen told me. "Daddy's taking her to the hospital. Come, I'll do your hair in braids like you like. You can use my yellow ribbons." This, more than anything, terrified me. I never got to use Helen's ribbons. She kept them on her dresser, laid out like museum pieces. If I ran my fingers along them to feel their satin surfaces, she would shake me by the shoulders. I didn't want to wear her ribbons. I wanted my mother back. But this time, she was gone too far away. I watched my father carry her down the steps and out to the car. His face as he drove away was as impassive as hers.

Things changed drastically after my mother went into the hospital. My father immediately hired a stout blond German woman named Anna to help out around the house. She was a spinster who sat on her porch and frowned at all of us children when our ball landed in her yard. She lived with her brother and his wife, two doors down from us. She had always smiled and waved at my father, secretly straightened the back of her dress when she stood talking to him. She didn't do well at holding jobs, as her brother seemed to enjoy pointing out. "Anna speaks her mind come hell or high water," he said. "She doesn't win many popularity contests." But she liked my father, and she was happy to take a job with us. "You girls behave for her," he told us. "I'm not paying her much of anything. We're lucky to have her."

Anna believed strongly in order and discipline. We ate regular meals at regular times. I remembered often the last meal my mother had made. It was hot outside, and she'd made fruit salad. When my father came home and saw what was on the dinner table, he'd said, *"Fruit salad?"* Mary, the youngest of us at five, said excitedly, "With whipped cream, Daddy!" He'd opened the refrigerator, scowling, and then left the house, slamming the door. My mother shrugged. "He's gone out for a steak," she said. "He'll just get hotter, I'll bet you." She pulled her blouse away from her chest. "It must be ninety-nine degrees. When it's like this, it is such a pleasure to eat something so cool. Don't you think?" "It's pretty, too," I'd said, and my mother had smiled at me. Later that night, I heard the screen door slam. Then I heard my mother's apologetic murmurs, and the short, angry sentences my father said back to her. He's still mad, I'd thought. Even after he's had his steak, he's still mad.

Now we had meat, potatoes, and a vegetable every night. We were to eat everything on our plates, clean them well enough to flip them over, and then efficiently have dessert on the other side. We no longer picked out our own clothes to wear—Anna chose an outfit for us each night before she went home. Although my teacher commented positively on my improved appearance, I didn't like having my clothes picked out. Nor did I like the influx of strangers into our house—friends of Helen's began coming over, and giggling with her behind closed doors.

When it was bath time, Anna made me stop whatever I was doing immediately. "Come now," she would say. "You wash like I told you—start with your hair, and work all the way to your toes. Don't forget anything in the middle. And hurry—there are others waiting." I used to stare into her ruddy, stiff face as she ordered me about, looking for a way to see into her. But there was no access for me. Her braids were wound so tightly around her head. Not a single hair was out of place—loose, blowing softly, and itself. I looked carefully, in front and behind, but everything was exactly in place.

While I grew more and more unhappy with this new arrangement, I noticed something about my father: he seemed more and more content. He smiled at me one night after dinner, patted his lap, and said, "Come here, Lizzy. Tell me what you did in school today."

I climbed onto him and said, "Mary misses Mama. She was crying today."

"Ah, well . . . I know. And you—what did you do in school? Numbers? Spelling?"

I heard the clatter of the dishes Anna was doing in the kitchen. I saw that my father's hair was neatly combed. I ran my fingers along the line of his part, and he pulled my hand away.

"Where is Mama?" I asked.

He stopped smiling. "She's in the hospital, Lizzy. You know that."

"When will she come home?"

He moved uncomfortably under me. "Get off me, now. You're getting fat!"

I climbed down, then asked again, "When will she come home?"

He sighed. "I don't know, Lizzy. The doctors are trying to help her."

"Does she miss us?"

"I'm sure she does."

"I want to see her."

He looked away from me. "Where are your sisters? Where did everyone go?"

I put my hand on his arm. "Can I see her?"

"Lizzy, it's not a place for little girls. I can't bring you there. They have rules. Why don't you draw her a picture? I'll go and see her tomorrow and bring it to her. She likes your pictures."

I considered this. "I will draw her a picture. But I want to give it to her."

I felt Anna's presence behind me, and then heard her voice. "You're first tonight, young lady. Up into the bathroom." I didn't move, and my father started to get up.

"No, Carl," Anna said. "I can do this. You read your paper."

I saw my father smile, and then he leaned back into his chair. "Go, Lizzy," he said. He began to read.

After my bath, I drew my mother a bouquet of flowers. They were all small blossoms, which I knew she liked best. "They seem so shy, don't you think?" she'd told me. "And inside, the most secret." I made them all different colors, even silver and gold. "For you," I wrote, "who I love, love, love. Love, Lizzy." I folded the picture into fours, then slid it under my nightgown. I lay on my stomach so that it would stay where I'd put it: next to my heart, like a promise being made.

That night, I dreamed that a flower grew out of my eye. I was astounded, and stared and stared at myself in the mirror. I knew it was impossible, but there it was: a thin, supple stem exploding into a deep purple blossom, with a glowing yellow center. It swayed delicately back and forth as I turned my head, trying to see the source, to understand where it came from. Then I reached up and picked it, and ran to tell my father that it had grown out of my eye. "Don't be ridiculous," he said. I stood before him defiantly, and grew another flower, from the same eye, which was even lovelier than the first. I picked it again, and handed it to him. "Here," I said. Behind me, my mother materialized—filmy, beautiful, and smiling. "You can see the connection, Carl, can't you?" she asked. "Look at the veins on the petals. Now see them on your eyelid. They are both part of the same thing." I awakened suddenly, feeling frightened and inspired both. I felt for the drawing and, finding it safely against my chest, held it there while I went to look in the bathroom mirror. I saw nothing but my familiar self. As I was returning to bed, I heard a woman's voice coming from downstairs. I crept into the living room and saw Anna sitting close to my father on the sofa. Her voice was low and thick sounding, and she was smiling. Then I saw my father reach out and touch along the side of her face. I was horrified. I had seen Anna as a kind of machine, a necessary evil we would have to endure until my mother came back to take over in her comfortable, haphazard way. Now it occurred to me that Anna was a woman, and that she saw my father as a man. I had seen Anna eat, and she was greedy and thorough. She and my father had been sitting in the dim light for who knew how long, alone. I cleared my throat and they both jumped and turned toward me. "It's time for you to go home," I told Anna.

My father, flushed, said, "Lizzy . . ."

Anna stood up. "Well, you are right, Lizzy. I have finished my work for the day. Now I am just talking to Carl before I leave. It is business for big people, and not little girls." She came toward me. "I will help you back to bed."

"I don't need any help," I said, and turned toward my father.

He paused, then rose and said, "Well . . . thank you, Anna. I'll see you on Monday."

I saw her eyebrows raise slightly. "All right, then, Carl," she said, and smiled at him. When she turned toward me, her smile was gone.

Early the next morning, I dressed and came into the kitchen, where my father was sitting at the table with his coffee. I was relieved that it was Saturday and I could talk to him alone. I held my drawing out toward him. "This is what I made for Mama," I said.

He looked at his watch. "It's so early, Lizzy. Why are you up already? Everyone else is sleeping." I nodded, agreeing. "Why don't you go back to bed? I'll bring your picture when I go to see your mama."

"I want to come."

He sighed. "You can't. I told you little girls can't come there."

"How do you know?"

He stared at me, exasperated. "If you come, your sisters will want to come, too. I can't bring so many."

"They don't want to come."

"I'm sure they do, Lizzy."

"No, they don't. I asked them. They don't want to come with me. They're scared. But I'm not."

He folded the newspaper. "All right, I'll bring you this time. But if they say you can't come in, you'll have to wait in the lobby by yourself. Can you do that?"

I said yes, because I was supremely confident that I wouldn't have to. I knew I would see my mother. She had come to me in my dream last night. She wanted to see me.

I played dolls with Mary until it was time to go. My good fortune was making me feel benevolent, and I let her lead. "Now we are going to the park," she said, and we took the dolls into the backyard.

"Now they get to the park," I said, "and it's a funny kind of sky and all of the sudden they see a bush with diamonds growing on it, and they pick them and buy a castle with alligators in the moat."

"No!" she said. "*I* say what! Now they see a bush and it has money all on it."

"All right," I said. "That's fine."

There was some reluctance on the part of the hospital staff to let me see my mother. But eventually, they said I could visit her if I would stay only ten minutes. I agreed readily, and then, holding my father's hand, went down the long hall toward my mother's room.

There were two narrow beds in her room. The one by the window was empty, and the one by the door held a woman who looked somewhat like my mother. She was motionless, lying on her back. Her eyes were open, though, and I was relieved to see that she looked at me when I came over to her. "Mama?" I said. "I came to see you. I brought you a drawing. It's of something you like." I held the paper toward her, and she began to weep. "Oh, no," I said. "Don't cry, Mama." I looked for help from my father, but he was standing far away, looking embarrassed. "See?" I said, opening the drawing. "It's flowers."

She smiled, and traced the outline of the blossoms with her fingers. Then she put her hand under my chin. I had forgotten the wonderful lightness of her touch, and I leaned toward her, missing her more at that moment than I had in all the time she'd been gone. "You are Lizzy, aren't you?" she asked. I was shocked at first, then embarrassed, like my father. But then I climbed up on the bed to sit beside her. "Yes I am," I said. "And you are the best mother. And soon you will come home, and we will have a party with paper plates."

"Yes." She sat up in bed and propped the pillow behind her. Then she looked up at my father. "Carl?"

He stepped forward.

She hesitated, closed her mouth, which had started to say something, and leaned back against the pillows to stare into his face for a long moment. Then she said in a low and carefully controlled voice, "I do want to come home."

I grew very excited. But my father said, "I don't think yet, Marion. The doctor said it would be a few more weeks, anyway."

She nodded, and looked down into her lap. Her hands looked thinner to me, her hair dull and unkempt. I didn't understand her compliance. Why didn't she simply get dressed and come with us, laugh gently at my father and ignore his protestations in the way she had always done before? A nurse came in and handed my mother a paper cup full of pills. She swallowed them without looking at them. "What was that?" I asked.

She shrugged, and answered in a flat voice, "I don't know."

I felt an area at the base of my throat hurt with sudden anger. "Why don't you come home today? Why don't you?"

My father stepped forward and took my hand. "We've got to go now, Lizzy. Tell your mother good-bye."

I pulled my hand away. "No."

"If you behave that way, you can't come back anymore."

"I don't care."

My mother reached out toward me. "Come here, Lizzy. I will tell you a secret."

I hesitated, then went to her. She brushed back my hair, and whispered in my ear, "I am with you still."

"No you're not," I said petulantly. "Big, fat Anna is."

She looked at my father. "The woman from down the street that helps out," he said. "I told you about her."

"Ah, yes," she said, and raised her chin in a way that made her look herself again, proud, a little careless, and remarkably beautiful. I had forgotten that. My mother was very beautiful. I put her hand to my mouth, kissed it loudly three times, and told her good-bye.

"I'll come again," I said.

She smiled at me. "Do," she said. "I will have something for you next time. Something from nothing. A treasure."

In the hall, on the way out, I said, "She's getting better."

My father stared straight ahead. "Maybe."

"Oh, she is," I said. "I can tell easy."

"Lizzy, last time I saw her, she didn't even speak. It's rare that she does."

"Well, you should have brought me."

"She's still sick, Lizzy. It's just hard for you to understand."

"She's getting better," I said.

When we got home, Helen called me into her room and closed the door. "What did she look like?" she asked.

I shrugged. "I don't know. Mama."

"Did she have pajamas on?"

"Yes, I guess so."

"Well, *think*, Lizzy! Did she look crazy?"

"What do you mean?"

Helen narrowed her eyes. "You know, did she say strange things? Or did she act regular?"

I thought about what "regular" might mean. Then I said, "She acted regular. And she wants to come home."

Helen sat on her bed and stared past me. Her mouth was a bitter straight line. "She can't come home until she can take care of us," she said. "I'll tell you that right now."

"She *can* take care of us!"

"I mean really take care of us. Like Anna does."

"Oh," I said. I walked over to Helen's bookshelf, where she kept her collection of glass figures.

"Don't touch anything," she said.

"I wasn't going to," I said. "I was just looking." But I was going to touch something, hard.

The weather began to grow cold, and Anna and my father took us shopping for coats. I rejected everything Anna suggested. "How about this one, Lizzy?" she would say, holding up a blue parka. "I hate blue more than anything," I would say, scarcely looking. "This one, then," she would say later, her tone assuming a bit of an edge. "No," I would say. "Well. Aren't we fussy!" Anna would say under her breath, and make a show out of helping her more accommodating charges. My father finally suggested a coat that I thought must have been made for a boy, but I took it happily. "Yes, this one," I said. "I like this one very, very much."

This kind of thing was not unusual. Anna and I fought quiet battles constantly. But Mary had grown used to Anna, sat happily on her lap, and was read to each evening after her hair had been brushed and admired. Helen enjoyed a kind of peer relationship with her—they planned dinner menus together, made lists of chores for Mary and me to do. And my father continued to smile his satisfied smiles. In addition to that, I had heard him with Anna again late at night, only this time in his bedroom. I'd stood outside the door, listening to their whispers and painful-sounding moans. I'd put my hand up to knock, but then changed my mind and went back to bed. I stared into the darkness for a long while, thinking of how I would save this information and use it later. Then the pain would have a purpose.

The next time my father went to visit my mother, I came along. She was in the dayroom, sitting in front of a television. When she saw me, she smiled and held out her arms. I ran to her and she said, "This is a such a good day, Lizzy! I get to come home for Thanksgiving!" My father seemed nervous with the information. "Are you sure?" he kept saying. Finally, my mother brought him over to the nurse behind the desk. "Tell him I get to come home," she said. "He's having difficulty with the concept." Then she leaned forward and added in a stage whisper, "Do you have a pill for him?" The nurse smiled begrudgingly.

I told Anna the news when we got home. "Guess what?" I said.

"What?" She sat down across the table from me but didn't look at me. She was waiting for my father to come into the room. Then she would pay careful attention to me. But when I said that my mother was coming home, I had her attention legitimately. "When?" she asked.

"Thanksgiving," I said. "We will have a big turkey and three pies. That's how we always do it. And my mother will cook," I added pointedly.

My father came into the kitchen, and Anna asked him if it was true. "Well, that's what they said today," he said. "Of course, it's a week away."

Anna stood up and slid the chair under the table. "Well, I suppose you won't be needing me after that, then."

My father reached out a hand toward her, then stopped it
midair. Anna looked at me. She was willing me to leave the room,
I knew. And because the larger victory was mine, I did. "I'm
awfully sorry if this hurts you," I heard my father saying.

"Oh Anna, I'm sorry if this hurts you," I mimicked on my way
up the stairs. I thrust open the door to Helen's room. She was
painting her nails with a deep pink polish, and her hair was up in
curlers. "Mama's coming home," I said. "Very soon," I added, staring into her surprised face. Mary, who shared the room with her,
jumped off her bed, where she'd been coloring, happily excited.

"You can come with me, Mary," I said. "We will make her a 'welcome home' card."

"Two," said Mary.

"Three," I said. "Three hundred and three."

My mother did make pies for Thanksgiving Day. But not three.
She made five. "One for each of us," she said. "This is a Thanksgiving much more special than any other. Five pies, for feeling five
times more thankful than ever. We'll make apple, cherry, pump-
kin, mince, and . . . what? Blueberry? Yes, blueberry. A whole pie
apiece. I'll put our names on top of them." She was flushed with
her intentions, bustling around the kitchen with her apron on.
She never used recipes, finding the notion of using the same
amount of ingredients each time ridiculous. "The humidity in the
air alone affects everything," she said. "You have to cook with
your senses. You pour in vanilla, smell, and see what you think."
She opened a drawer, then asked, "What are these measuring
spoons doing here?"

"They are Anna's," Helen told her, stiffly. "And she's a very good cook."

"Well, I'm sure she is," my mother said. "But Helen, you must know: there is cooking, and then there is . . ." She looked up, searched the ceiling for her meaning. Then she simply spread her arms, shrugged her shoulders, and said, *"Real* cooking." She insisted that we all help. Helen, scowling a little, rolled out dough. "Love it as you do it," my mother said, "or it will fall right apart." I shook various spices into various bowls until the smell was right to both of us. Mary stirred relentlessly, her eyebrows nearly meeting in her concentration. My father was assigned to pour our mixes into the pie shells and crimp the second crusts, but he deferred to my mother.

"Go ahead," he said, from his vantage point at the kitchen table. "You know I can't cook."

"Oh, Carl," she said. "You can! But if you let the food know you're afraid of it, it will turn on you." She was being charming, and she looked wonderful. At one point, she sat on his lap and kissed him, leaving the residue of flour in the form of handprints on either side of his face. He seemed pleased, and colored nicely. I made up a hasty prayer, thanking God for his nick-of-time intervention.

Before our efforts went into the oven, my mother made us stand before them. "Be serious, now," she said. And then she addressed the straight line of beautiful raw pies. "We appreciate your sacrifice," she said. "We thank you and the earth you came from. Amen." Then she opened the door with a flourish.

"Marion," my father said.

She turned toward him expectantly.

"What about the turkey?"

"Oh Carl!" she laughed. "How can you fit turkey in when you'll have a whole pie?"

This seemed a perfectly sensible answer to me, but I saw his face darken, and Helen's too. But Mary, my mother, and I, we were dizzy with happiness. It was Thanksgiving; Mama was home, and the pies filled the house with smells so seductive you eventually leaned back, smiled, and thought about them alone, nothing else, no matter who you were. It was a matter of really being somewhere. It was a matter of paying attention, my mother's forte.

About a week after my mother had been home, I woke up at night and heard her arguing with my father. "I said I'd make sure you took them!" he said.

"Carl, I don't need them," she said. "They make me tired."

"You do need them. They made you better, and you need them to stay well. The doctor said it's very important not to miss a dose."

"Well, I've missed three days' worth," she said. "Do I seem unwell to you?" Then, again, in a different kind of voice, she said, "Do I?" Then it was quiet, and I was content.

At the end of another week, however, my mother did seem unwell. She would start sentences, then wave them away, unfinished. I came home from school one day to find her sitting alone and staring. It was frighteningly familiar. "Mama?" I asked. "Are you all right?"

To my great relief, she turned to me and smiled. But it was a sad smile, and what she said was, "Oh, Lizzy. I just don't know." Within three days, she was back in the hospital again, worse, my father said, and Anna was back with us. We were instructed to remember how much she'd done for us. I remembered instead what she'd taken from us. I vowed not to speak to her. If the house caught on fire, I'd point. If she chose not to look, it was too bad.

Because I would not hear otherwise, my father took me with him to see my mother again. She'd had what he called shock therapy, and she had a great deal of difficulty with her memory. "I made you something," she said, "and I don't know where it is."

"You'll find it," I said. And then, "What is it, anyway?"

She pushed my hair back from my face. "Animals."

"Oh," I said. I had no idea what she was talking about. And sometimes, if you pushed her for more information, she would cry in frustration. I prayed with my fists clenched, I made her many drawings, I visited her often; but she worsened.

Anna had resumed her duties with a wounded air, but her affection for my father remained. Therefore she appeared grimly at our door each morning, and lingered hopefully each evening. He was kind, but seemed to have lost any romantic interest in her. Helen was just as happy to have our mother gone again, and Mary seemed to have accepted the concept of alternating mothers as a comfortable enough norm. "Mama's totally crazy, you know," Helen told me one night. "She always has been. And she just keeps getting worse and worse. Now she's not ever going to be able to come home."

"That's what you think," I said.

"That's what I know. For God's sake, Lizzy. Aren't you ever embarrassed about her?"

This had not occurred to me. And now, I swallowed dryly and said, "No. You embarrass me."

"Oh, sure," she said. "How do I embarrass you?"

"Your lies," I said, and walked away.

"What are you even talking about?" she shouted. "You're just like her! You don't even make sense!"

I closed my door quietly. I wanted to think about why I would ever be embarrassed about my mother, whom I trusted above everyone, who revealed things magical and satisfying, who held me close to her and sang songs I'd never heard while I breathed in her plain and lovely flesh smell.

One day, on the way to the hospital, my father said, "Well, they said they were going to try something new this morning."

"What?" I asked.

"It's called insulin shock."

This sounded worse than ever. "Why?" I asked.

"Because," he said, "when something doesn't work, you've got to try something else."

"Oh." I looked out the window. I wished the hospital were closer. It was a long drive, and I was tired of it. When we got there, my father was called over to the desk. I went on to my mother's room, not seeing her in the dayroom. It was empty. I sat on a chair and looked around, waiting. I saw something lying on the windowsill and went to investigate. It was a giraffe, made from straw wrappers twisted together—a kind of three-dimensional drawing. Next to it was an elephant, with ruffled, expansive ears. My mother had often told me that these were her favorite animals. "Oftentimes when a giraffe falls, it can't get back up again. Think of it, living a life where balance is so essential! And still, they look so graceful and carefree, nuzzling the tops of trees, looking down on us all." Elephants she admired for their human-like traits. "They get very happy when they see each other. Even if it's only been a little while, they carry on so—trumpeting and stomping all over the place. And here is something truly extraordinary about elephants: they seem to know they die. Oh, how unlucky they are, to be hunted for their ivory when their living minds are so wonderful. Tell me," she'd said, "what sight is better than a baby elephant holding on to its mother's tail?" "I don't know," I'd said. "I can't think of anything."

"Not anything?" she'd teased.

I knew what she meant. "Me holding on to you!" I'd said. "Right?"

"No," she'd said, suddenly serious. "Me holding on to you." She'd reached down and hugged me tightly. "It's me who holds on to you."

I heard a noise behind me and jumped. It was my father, who looked pale and nervous. "Lizzy, come here," he said.

"Look what Mama made," I said. "These are the animals she was talking about."

"Lizzy," he said, and his voice cracked, and I knew.

I stood up straight and made my insides be quite still. "She's dead," I said. "Isn't she?"

He nodded miserably.

"Why?" I asked.

"The insulin," he said. "She got too much. It happens sometimes. They called just after we left the house. Ah, Lizzy," he said. "She was so beautiful. She used to be so beautiful."

I turned toward the animals. "I want these," I said. "These are mine." He nodded. I picked them up, and they fell out of alignment, lost their shapes. At first I was filled with remorse. How could I ever fix them? But then she came to me, and I remembered what I knew, and I wasn't afraid. I knew what was gone, but I knew what would stay.

White Dwarf

If you were to ask Phyllis if her marriage was in trouble, she would answer this way: "Well, of course it is. Why do you think I spend so much time in the laundry room? Why do you think I sigh and sigh this way? Of course it is!" If you were to ask George, he would say, "Is it in *trouble*? Why, I don't believe so. You'd have to ask Phyllis, I guess. What do you mean, exactly, 'in trouble'?"

There was no fighting. Their life worked: their children fought and laughed with each other, did well in school, confessed readily to small crimes they committed, and endured with equanimity the small punishments for same. They knew this: if you were sent to your room, pretty soon everyone would join you up there anyway, lie on your bed and chat about things, forgive you.

George and Phyllis exchanged necessary news of the day, smiled at their children's inadvertent charm, watched television together in bed at night. Occasionally they had sex, although the last time they tried George looked up from kissing Phyllis's stomach to find her staring at the ceiling and silently weeping. "For God's sake, what's wrong with *you*?" he'd asked, rolling away from her. She had reached for a Kleenex to blow her nose, relieved, in a way. "I don't know," she said, and then, again, "I don't know." George bit at his lower lip. "Are you tired or something?" Phyllis sighed and nodded. George turned on channel seven to catch the weather.

It was Phyllis's idea to take a trip together. She felt guilty about crying while George tried to make love to her. She'd tried to tell her girlfriend about it. "It felt like, I don't know . . . It felt like *rape.*" Her friend gave her the name of a good woman therapist who took Blue Cross. Phyllis wrote it down and then threw it away. She decided a trip would do it. Time alone, and they'd get to know each other again. It was written about in all the women's magazines. You had to make your marriage a priority, spend a little time together. They would send the girls to George's mother's house. Then they would go to an inn by the ocean for three days. Something would happen there. Things would get better. "Why, George!" Phyllis would say, over wine by the fireplace. *"George!"* She would be glowing a little, look kind of pretty.

George took the kids to his mother's while Phyllis finished packing. She had kissed their foreheads, looked into their eyes seriously, promised to bring them something—clothes for the twelve-year-old, a stuffed animal for the eight-year-old. "Okay, okay!" they said, and pulled away. They were ready to stay up late, eat sweets for breakfast—they liked staying with Grandma.

Phyllis lined the suitcases up by the front door. When George came back, she pointed to them. "All set," she said. Her voice had lost some vitality—she was nervous. George nodded. She carried out the small one; he took the bigger two. He complained a little—"What's *in* here?"—but it was rather flirtatious, and Phyllis thought, Already it's better. Those magazines are absolutely right.

They drove for a while, talked about how the kids would do. Then it seemed there was nothing to say. It felt like diving into a shallow pond, hitting your head on a bottom you thought was far away. Phyllis felt it was her responsibility to think of something to say, since the trip had been her idea. She wanted to be entertaining. She asked George, "Say you had no money, and you found someone's wallet who was loaded. I mean, there were hundreds and hundreds of dollars in there—the thing was just bulging. Would you take out any money before you returned it?"

"No."

The brevity of his response disappointed her. He didn't understand what she was trying to do. "No, I mean . . . Well, suppose your mother was starving. Or dying. Or both."

He looked at her severely. "No, Phyllis. I wouldn't take any money." Then he returned his gaze to the road, shifted in his seat uncomfortably. I know where he wishes he was, she thought—not with me. Somewhere else. Work, or alone. She remembered the print she'd shown him recently that she'd wanted for the living room. He'd said nothing, stood far away from it, jangled change in his pocket. She'd said, "Well, I mean, I just liked those colors . . . ," and then stopped, humiliated. They hadn't bought it.

She turned to look out the window and considered the possibility that she was being oversensitive, unfair. Perhaps she *should* see someone, a therapist in some peaceful office. But she didn't know how that could work. They would be, after all, only two human beings. She would sit in a chair with pain expanding inside her. She would try to talk about it, and cry. The therapist would hand her Kleenex. At the end, Phyllis would write out a check in the amount equivalent to a cartful of groceries. She doubted she'd feel better. She thought she'd end up saying she would like to stop coming. "I don't see that you really figure anything out here," she would say.

She sighed, a small sound, and stared out the window at the landscape. There was nothing to see, really. George had taken the interstate, dismissing Phyllis's suggestion to take the more scenic route. "That way is hours longer," he'd said. "Let's just get there." She looked at his profile, saw, surprised, a certain softening around his chin. Midlife, she thought, and the word seemed foreign to her, made up, an object she could hold away from herself and look at.

It bothered her how George could be so comfortable with their silence. They could say anything now! She wanted to know about him. She remembered her girlfriend telling about something she did with license plates: "Let the letters you see suggest a phrase to you," she'd said. "You'd be surprised at what you come up with. You find out what's *really* going on in your head. No kidding—just try it." Phyllis looked at the plate on the car ahead of them. DTH, it said, and Phyllis thought, Don't Think Hard. She saw LBU and thought, Left Best Unsaid. She smiled a little. She started to tell George to try it, but then didn't. She waited for more plates. She saw MNL and thought, Maybe Now Leave. Then she thought, My God, I think she's right. She saw ADI and MHI and thought, All Day Insane and Me Hurt Inside.

"George," she said.

"Yeah." His face was calm, open. He was being friendly.

"Lisa told me this thing, about license plates. That if you look at them and make phrases out of the letters you see, it will tell you what's going on in your mind."

"I know what's going on in my mind. I'm starving."

"No, I mean subconsciously. I just did it, and it's true. Try it."

He looked at the MHI plate and said, "My Home Intact." Neither of them said anything at first, and then Phyllis swallowed and said, "Uh-huh."

He said, again, "I'm starving," and she said, "Then let's find a place to eat. I could eat."

IJG passed on the back of a blue station wagon. I Just Groan, she thought. She saw MYY on a red Honda Civic and thought, My Yearning Yells. She laughed a little. George looked at her and said, "What?"

She shook her head. It was nothing, her gesture said. An accident. PDT she saw. Please Don't Tell.

They pulled into the parking lot of a restaurant: a low, white building, red-and-white gingham curtains, hand-lettered signs, huge trucks parked at manly angles off to the side. Phyllis was pleased. She liked places like this, and they were hard to find anymore. "Maybe they'll have meat loaf," she told George. He reached for her hand, and she felt a rush of displeasure. She pulled away to rummage in her purse. "Want a mint?" she asked.

He looked at her. "We're going in to *eat*, Phyllis."

They sat at a corner table. Phyllis looked out the window. Cars were lined up, license plates all in a row. At the end was a battered pickup truck, MPL 709. My Poor Life, she thought. Many Problems Living. She looked at George reading the menu, studied his hands. His left thumbnail was deformed from a peach can falling on it when he was seven. She knew this about him. His hair was thinning in a small, cruel circle at the back of his head, and he ached about it. She knew that too. She heard the crunch of gravel as a car left the lot and looked at its plate. NKA 746. Never Know Another, she thought, and then thought, Won't I? Something inside her crumpled, fell in on itself. I *will* see a therapist, she thought. Something is so wrong.

They ordered cheeseburgers, onion rings, and chocolate shakes. They were being bad together, and it was fun. She knew every pair of socks he owned. They ate routinely from each other's plate. They had made two children together, astonishing cellular miracles, the best things in their lives—they had done this together. George had been there when each girl had been born, had seen them recoil at the sudden brightness of life, had heard them wail with tiny, trembling jaws, had seen their chests rise evenly as they breathed alone for the first time. But even then, Phyllis thought, even then there was this missing of each other. George hadn't cried, not even the first time. He'd looked embarrassed; and though he sat next to her it was as though the essence of himself was across the room, staring out the window. Phyllis had hidden the few tears she'd shed, kissed George on the cheek as he left, reminded him to let the dog out. It was after he was gone that she'd unwrapped the baby. She'd caressed the tightly clenched fists, the apricot cheeks. She'd traced the whorl of hair at the back of her daughter's head, watched the rhythm of her heartbeat in the soft spot. "I am your mother," she'd said. And then she cried freely, happily, staring in grateful disbelief at the size of the baby's toes.

Recently Phyllis had had a brief affair. All the time, the man said things to her like this: "I want your presence. I want your being. I want you to brush up against me in the hall in the house where we live." He told her her collarbones were beautiful; he kissed the gums above her teeth, telling her he wanted to be everywhere on her. He read poetry to her, fed her slices of fresh fruit. Her love for him was huge, frightening, and invigorating, but she quit the affair for the way her children looked asleep, and for the touching hole in George's underwear that she found on the day she was going to tell him she wanted out. But she missed that man. Sometimes his memory would spear her, and she would need to take a deep breath to keep on.

George was making noise with his straw. She looked at him, wondered if he had ever had a lover. She could ask him. But if she asked him, he would ask her, and then what? Their relationship was like a complicated arrangement of pickup sticks. Who wanted to go first? It was too dangerous.

Still, she wanted something. She said, "Know what I read the other day? That there was this mystery out in the country: A man found a house sparrow, decapitated. Then there were four more found, all by other people. Everyone was really upset, and they called ornithologists and everything, but no one could explain it. Then some guy saw one day what was happening: a grackle did it—just pecked at the necks of the sparrows until their heads came off."

George pushed away his plate. "Jesus."

She sighed, leaned forward. "Oh, I'm sorry. I just mean, my God, isn't it incredible? Why do you think he did that?"

"Well, he cracked up. I suppose birds do that, too."

"But it's so unsettling if birds go crazy, too. It makes everything so untrustworthy."

"Everything *is* untrustworthy. Anything can happen, at any time." He seemed so cold saying this. She wondered what he was telling her.

"What do you mean?"

"What do you mean what do I mean?" He signaled for the check. "The world is imperfect, Phyllis. You always forget."

They got back into the car. "Do the license plate thing with me," Phyllis said. She wanted to know.

George snorted lightly, then pointed to a black Saab. "Okay, T-I-N. Telling Is Nothing." Time Is Now, she thought. "F-N-W," he pointed to next. "First, Never Whine." Find New Woman, she thought.

He got back onto the freeway, put on the radio, turned the volume low. "Did you see what Rach was studying last night? About stars. She wants a telescope. I think we'll get her one."

"Don't you think they're too expensive?"

"Just a little one, used."

"Okay." She stared out the window, bit at her lip. Then she turned off the radio and said, "You know, Rachel told me about this one kind of star, a white dwarf. It collapses inward."

"Yeah, I know."

You don't know, she thought. Oh, no you don't. "I feel like that star, George." There. She'd said it.

"What do you mean?"

"I feel like I'm collapsing inward. Like the star."

"Jesus, Phyllis! Can't we ever just have a good time?"

She examined her fingernails, held her breath. Here was the moment. She thought of her lover standing in the middle of his kitchen in his flannel shirt and brown corduroy pants, stroking her hair and telling her she didn't even know how beautiful she was. Then she thought of Rachel reading about the stars, sighing contentedly before sleep, both of her parents in the room right next to hers.

"Where do you think we could get a telescope?" she asked.

"I don't know—we'll look in the paper, I guess."

A Porsche passed them, going fast. She saw the plate before it roared ahead. It was a funny one, a triple letter. NNN 733. Never, Never, Never, she thought, aching. "Hey, look," George said. "No News Nearing."

"Right," she said. She thought of the star being polite, sparing the universe the wreckage of its destruction. She thought of the grackle, its brain off-kilter, its own kind of destruction no better understood. She leaned back in her seat and closed her eyes.

George cleared his throat. "Phyllis?"

"What?"

"Please don't leave me."

She opened her eyes. He was staring straight ahead, immobile. She said nothing for a while, then wondered if she'd heard him correctly. "What did you say, George?"

"I asked you not to leave me."

"Well, I . . . I'm not going to."

"I know it's hard for you," he said.

"Do you?"

"Yes."

She turned to face him. "You know, George, so much would be helped if you'd just *talk* to me."

"Well. Men don't talk."

"Some men do."

He was quiet then. His face hardened, the air in the space between them seemed to change, and she understood that he knew. She made a small gesture with her hand toward him. "I'm sorry, George. It's over, you know."

"I know. For a while now."

"Yes."

"I didn't see any point in discussing it, Phyllis. These things happen."

She nodded, looked out the window. She saw a huge field of flowers. They were tall, an impossibly beautiful purple color. They grew straight toward the sun, sure of themselves. Phyllis thought about saying she wanted to stop and pick a bouquet for their room, but she knew George would object. *Let's just get there.* But then, at that moment, he pulled over, got out of the car, and went into the field. He picked several flowers, handed them to her through her open window with a shy flourish. "Here," he said. His feet were sinking slowly in the black mud.

He climbed into the car and started driving again. He wouldn't look at her. Phyllis stared into the center of one of the flowers. There were four fragile filaments, arching up, leaning forward, expectant. She felt her eyes fill with tears and she closed her lids against them.

"I made this snow tunnel once," George said.

She looked at him. "Pardon?"

"I said I made this snow tunnel once. The winter I turned eleven, it snowed about three feet. Alan Hirschfelt and I dug this really long tunnel in my backyard. It was freezing out— our moms made us wear those dopey hats with earflaps and chin straps and we were mad as hell about it. It took us hours to make that tunnel. We met in the middle just before it got dark. The snow looked blue. We were so excited when we were done— no breaks, just one long, perfect tunnel. We met right in the middle."

"So what did you do?" Phyllis asked.

"What do you mean?

"I mean when you were finished, what did you *do*?"

"Why, we shook hands. I remember that. We shook hands and then we went home."

"Oh," Phyllis said. She took in a breath. "I appreciate your telling me that, George. I like those kinds of stories very much."

"Okay." He turned the radio on, and she closed her eyes again. When she felt his hand over hers, she pushed her fingers up to slide between his. She had memorized his knuckles long ago, but the feeling now was quite new—full of hope, she realized, and full, too, of the exquisite relief of forgiveness.

The Matchmaker

The summer I turned eleven, I played matchmaker. I wanted Anna Gunther, the seventy-five-year-old woman to whom I tried to teach English, and Artie Miller, the seventy-six-year-old man who lived down the street, to fall in love. My intentions were not entirely philanthropic. If Anna and Artie worked, I thought I might learn enough about love to garner the affections of Billy Croucher, in whom I was newly and greatly interested. He was a class ahead of me in school, a fine baseball player, and indisputably handsome. He never paid any attention to me, though I played baseball nearly as well as he; but I believed that at any moment something would break through inside him, and he would see me clear. Then we would sit together on the bus. The notion of his hand resting on the seat near mine was enough to alter my breathing pattern.

Right after school was out, I got my Junior Scientist of America card in the mail. I wrapped it in Saran wrap and put it in a prominent place in my red plastic wallet. Then I ventured forth into the natural world, a recognized member of the scientific community at last, looking for important work. Sometimes I cracked open rocks, searching for elaborate crystal patterns. Sometimes I followed insects—secretly, I thought—to find out what they *really* did. Mostly, I gathered things to stare at under my microscope. The best things were always specimens from inside, though: salt crystals, sugar crystals, a hair from my head. Often I would look quickly from the eyepiece to the object on the slide, to make sure nobody was fooling me. How could those translucent, multidimensional blocks I saw in the microscope really be the same sugar I so casually sprinkled on my oatmeal?

In time, I grew tired of playing scientist. My best friend, Carol Conroy (who was my best friend mostly because she was an only child and therefore fascinating to me), had gone to Seattle on vacation. My other friend, the untidily overweight Kathy O'Connor, was not speaking to me due to the seriousness of our last argument, which had to do with whether or not playing waitress was babyish.

Anna Gunther came to me at exactly the right time: I needed a new project and a new friend. I first saw her when I emerged from some bushes where I'd been trying to catch a baby rabbit. He had eluded me, and I was hot and frustrated. She was sitting on the back porch of her house wearing a print sundress, sandals with short black socks, and a kerchief on her head.

"Hi," I said.

She smiled and nodded.

"I almost caught a baby rabbit," I said.

Again she smiled and nodded. I came in for a closer view. "You live there?" I asked.

She smiled yet again, and made some motion that indicated that she didn't understand me. I noticed her legs were unshaven. "No English?" I asked.

She nodded happily. "No English. No English."

I grew very excited. I'd never met anyone who didn't speak English before. I licked my lips and stood up straighter. I pointed to myself. "Sarah," I said. And then again, "Sarah."

"Sarah," she repeated, and then, pointing to herself, she said, "Anna."

"Anna," I said, and she beamed.

This was going very well, I thought. "I teach you English?" I asked, and she stared blankly at me. I wondered how to pantomime "teach." We studied each other in friendly expectation. Then I picked up a rock. "Rock," I said, pointing to it.

"Rock," she answered seriously.

"Yes!" I said, and picked up a stick.

We went on that way for some time. It never occurred to me that she might not want to be doing this. At one point, a younger woman came to the door and spoke in German to Anna. Then she looked at me and said, "Hello. You're teaching my mother English?"

I blushed. "Well . . ."

"That's fine," she said. "My mother just came here from Stuttgart a week ago—she doesn't know any English. And she loves children."

She spoke German to her mother again, and Anna nodded enthusiastically. I'm hired, I thought.

I came over to Anna's back porch each afternoon. She would be waiting for me with a plate of cookies. We would have a little treat together, and then commence our lesson of the day. I thought it was important for Anna to learn animals, because I liked them. I brought over a huge volume depicting wildlife, and we would look at the pictures together. "Tiger," I would say, pointing. "Boa constrictor." Sometimes she would tell me the names of the animals in German, and when I haltingly repeated them back, she would nod approvingly.

One day as I was preparing to go to Anna's, I noticed that my turtle was looking sickly. I'd forgotten to feed him the day before, and I wasn't sure I'd remembered the day before that, either. In addition to that, his water had nearly all evaporated. I felt terrible. I filled his bowl with fresh water and gave him a generous serving of assorted fly parts, and brought him with me to Anna's.

She was properly concerned when I managed to communicate that the turtle was sick. (This I had done by making retching sounds while pointing to the turtle.) She picked him up and laid him gently on her skirt and stroked his tiny head on the diamond-shaped depression between his eyes. If turtles sigh, he did then. She spoke a little German to him, soft, incomprehensible words of comfort, and put him back by his plastic palm tree. Then she turned her attention to me to begin learning the names of wild-flowers.

The next morning, I found the turtle dead. I cried about it to my mother, who was kind enough to not point out that it was all my fault; and she gave me a velvet-lined jewelry box to be the turtle's casket. I put him in the box, gave him a kiss good-bye, and took him outside to bury him. It seemed to me that a turtle who had been so much abused in life ought to be buried in a magnificent place as compensation. The best place I knew was the gully, a large valley near my house where I would often play. The grass was eye high there, and rich smelling. There was a stream that ran through it, with water so clear it was almost invisible, and with smooth stones and patches of moss all along the banks. I thought it would be good to have the turtle overlook the stream, to be high up on a hill with the sunshine while the water ran steadily below. I found a rock suitable for digging and had just begun when I was suddenly overwhelmed with grief. I dropped the rock and covered my face with my hands. I wasn't done with that turtle—why did he have to die? Did he hurt when he died? Did he hold a grudge against me? When he got to heaven and God asked him how it had gone, would he say, "Oh, it was fine until Sarah Harris starved me to death"?

"*Sarah Harris?*" God would say.

Oh, it was terrible. Pain and neglect were in the world, and suffering; but when it was *your fault* . . . I wept.

I was interrupted by the sound of someone clearing his throat. I looked up to see an older man wearing corduroy pants, a blue shirt, and a cardigan sweater. He had slippers on, too, the kind my dad wore.

"Lose a pet?" he asked.

I nodded miserably.

"What kind?"

"A turtle," I said. "He was from the dime store."

The man nodded and began helping me dig. "I used to have a turtle," he said, and I thought that he sounded sad. This seemed a fitting enough tribute for a turtle, to have two people thinking sorrowful and kind thoughts about him at the same time, one even an adult, and I began to feel better.

"You live here?" I asked the man.

"About half a block down the street from you."

I was surprised. "I've never seen you."

"My wife was sick for a long time," he said. "I couldn't get out much—busy taking care of her."

"Is she okay now?"

"She died."

My eyes widened. A turtle was one thing, but a person! "Oh!" I said. "That's sad."

He looked down at me and smiled. "We had a good life together," he said.

I patted the turtle's grave. "My grandpa died," I said. "But I didn't know him. He was seventy-six."

"So am I," the man said.

I felt extremely awkward. "My other grandpa is eighty," I said. "He's still alive."

"What's your name?" the man asked. I told him and asked him his. "Artie Miller," he said, and shook my hand. It made me feel very grown-up, and I decided I liked him.

"Would you like to meet a woman your age?" I asked.

"I don't think so," he said. "Not yet."

"She doesn't speak English. She lives on the block next to ours."

"Maybe another time. Okay?"

"Okay." I watched him go.

"Hearts," I said to Anna the next afternoon. I had an Archie comic book and I was showing Anna the hearts that came out of Betty when she watched Archie walk by. Archie didn't even notice Betty, besotted the way he was with the raven-haired Veronica.

"Hearts," Anna said dutifully.

I pointed to my chest. "My heart," I said.

Anna pointed to her ample bosom. "My-heart," she said.

"Yes. Very good," I said, and then rose, indicating a transition. I pointed again to my chest, saying, "Heart?" Then I fluttered my eyelashes and sighed and said, "Love."

Anna seemed not to understand me.

I embraced the air, closed my eyes, and made loud kissing sounds. Then I opened my eyes and said in a dreamy voice, "Loooovvvve."

"*Acht!*" she said. "Love! *Ja!*"

Her face softened. She knew what I meant. That was enough of that for today. It never paid to rush a fragile thing. I pulled a pile of my favorite baseball cards from my jeans pocket and sat beside her. "Minnesota Twins," I said.

Anna selected a chocolate cookie from the plate between us. "Minn-ah-so-ta," she said carefully, and took a bite. Then, "Twins!" she said triumphantly.

"Perfect!" I said.

Kathy O'Connor came to my door the next morning and stared sullenly at me. "Do you want to make up?"

I shrugged. "Okay." I came outside and we sat on the grass in front of my house to discuss what we might do. Kathy wanted to play the Barbie game, but I thought this could easily lead to trouble. The object of the game was to "win" the handsome Ken as your date to the prom. The problem was that I preferred the bespectacled Tom, who I assumed was vastly more intelligent than Ken and therefore better equipped to appreciate my charms, which were not entirely visible to the casual observer. Kathy thought that if you weren't trying to win Ken, you were cheating. I had once suggested that we both try to win Tom, but it was no good—Kathy pointed to the rules printed on the box top, her lips whitely pressed together. As our relationship was in the delicate healing process, I suggested we stay outside. "Want to play Indian?" I asked.

She thought about it for a while, staring off into the distance while I did cartwheels to loosen up. Then she agreed, and we went to the gully, to the tepee. Carol Conroy and I had, after Christmas, gathered many of the neighbors' thrown-out trees and brought them to the gully to construct living quarters next to the stream. The house occasionally fell down, and constantly lost needles; but on the whole it functioned quite well. It was mainly background anyway, as the bulk of our time was spent foraging for food. After elaborate searches, we would always end up with the same fare: red berries wrapped in green leaves, which were then speared onto a stick and roasted over our "campfire."

While Kathy and I were busy cooking that day, I noticed the sun getting higher in the sky, and remembered Anna. "I've got to go," I said.

"Where?" Kathy asked, annoyed. She was bending over the circle of rocks that made our campfire, trying to stabilize our spit, two Y-shaped twigs. I told her about Anna. "But I want to stay down here some more," she said. "Come on."

"You can stay," I said. "I want to go."

She rose up and the twigs fell down. "I can't stay," she said petulantly. "I can't be down here alone."

"Why not?" I had spent hours in the gully alone, did some of my best thinking there.

"Because there are bad boys down here," she said. "My mom told me."

One reason that Kathy O'Connor could never be my best friend was that she was always saying ridiculous things like that. Just when you were having a fine time, she'd say something like if you swallowed an orange seed, you could die.

"You can stay here, Kathy," I said. "There are no bad boys. I have to go."

She sighed loudly and followed me out of the gully, maintaining enough distance to clearly communicate her anger. Appar-

ently we were at it again. I didn't mind. Anna was more interesting than playing Indians with Kathy, who never did it right anyway. It was Carol Conroy who was a good Indian, probably
because, as she so often pointed out, she was *part* Indian. "My
mother is a Cherokee," Carol once told me. "They can cut stone
with their fingernails." I had great respect for Carol's mother after
that, and maintained a respectful silence around her.

Anna was happy to see me. I had brought no teaching aides
along today, and she seemed surprised. But I had a plan. I knew
that Artie Miller took daily afternoon walks. I'd seen him often
after our meeting at the funeral. I hoped to arrange an "accidental"
meeting between the two of them. I was pleased to see that Anna
looked very nice that day, with her hair braided and pinned up
over her head and with her foreign, dangling earrings reflecting
the sunlight whenever she moved.

"Hello, Anna," I said. "Today"—here I raised my eyebrows
expectantly—"a walk!"

She waited for me to explain. "A walk," I said, and demonstrated,
walking purposefully around in a circle, taking deep breaths and
exhaling vigorously. I held out my arm to her invitingly.

"Okay!" She opened the back door to yell something in German to her daughter, who yelled back, *"Gut! Gut!"* and then we
were off.

I pointed out and named things for Anna. "Sidewalk," I said,
and patted it with my sneaker. "Sun," I said, and we both squinted
upward. "Tree," I pointed, and then sprang a pop quiz. "This?" I
asked, pointing to the sidewalk.

Anna stopped walking to concentrate. "Zeit. Walk," she said.

"Good. But *side*. Sidewalk."

"Okay," she said agreeably. "Zide. Zidewalk."

As we neared the end of the block, I saw Artie emerging from his front door. Oh, this was perfect. I was so good at this. I looked at Anna out of the corner of my eye. She was looking at Artie. This would be too easy.

"Man," I said casually. Anna nodded. She knew that one. "I *know* that man," I said. Anna looked at me uncomprehendingly. "Anna and Sarah," I said, and shook hands with her. I pointed to Artie, and made another shaking motion. "*Artie* and Sarah."

"*Ja,*" she said. Anna was very smart, I thought proudly. We walked closer, and Artie recognized me and waved.

"Hello, Sarah!" I thought he looked a little nervous, but I was pleased to see that he was wearing his blue cardigan.

"Hi, Artie. I'm just taking a walk with my friend Anna, here. She doesn't speak English. Remember?"

He nodded to Anna and said to me, "I remember."

I stood between them to make my introduction. "Artie," I said, pointing to him. "Anna," I said, pointing to her. They shook hands, and Anna nodded a few times, smiling. I saw she was blushing a little, and took this as a good sign. Artie was smiling at her.

Then he turned to me and said, "I was just about to go for a walk."

"I know," I said. "I see you every day."

"Yes, well . . ." He looked at Anna again. "Nice to meet you," he said, and then, "Welcome to America!"

He walked away. Anna looked at me expectantly. "And now— we walk home," I said, and turned her around. I thought the meeting had gone very well. I was learning much about making love happen—surely Billy Croucher would be mine by September. I'd seen him riding his bike through the neighborhood three times thus far. Twice he had spoken to me, and one of those times had accepted a Life Saver.

Anna and I passed Kathy O'Connor sulking on her front porch on the way back. I didn't want her to do anything that would discredit me in Anna's eyes, and I gave her a friendly wave. "Is that her?" she called out.

"Yes," I said. "Want to meet her?"

Kathy did her usual hesitating, and then clomped down her steps to come and stand critically before Anna, who smiled at her and extended her hand, saying, "Hello. *Ich Anna.*"

Kathy shrugged and shook Anna's hand. "I'm Kathy," she said. "Can't you speak English?"

Anna looked at me, then back at Kathy. "Zidewalk," she said.

Kathy snorted, and pointed derisively at me. *"She's* not an English teacher!"

Anna smiled, thinking she understood. *"Ja*—teacher," she said fondly.

"What does 'How do you do?' mean?" Kathy challenged her. "How about 'One, two, three'?"

Anna stopped smiling. "Shut up, Kathy," I said, quietly.

"You haven't taught her anything. She can't understand anything. She's a moron."

I took Anna's arm and smiled pleasantly at Kathy. "Okay," I said. "Good. Good-bye, now." We began walking.

Kathy stood on the sidewalk watching us go. "You're so *stupid!"* she yelled after us. I turned and waved.

"Okay—see you later."

Back at Anna's, I decided to open up. "Kathy?" I asked. Anna nodded. *"Stinky,"* I said, holding my nose. "P.U."

Anna nodded gravely. *"Ja,* P.U.," she said. "Okay."

I played alone in the gully the next morning. I caught a grasshopper and stared at him through a crack in my fingers while I held him in my closed hand. He was frightened, and alternated between struggling desperately and holding extremely still. I felt sorry for him, but I wanted to take in a little more of his fine anatomy before I set him free. When I let him loose, he remained still for a moment, as though stunned by his good fortune. Then he sprang up high, exhilarated, and was gone. I lay down in the grass and opened my eyes wide. Here was a forest, miniature and pliant, and here was I, godlike. I watched ants, serious minded and marching in a row. I heard the complicated sound of whirring insect wings close by, but I couldn't see what the insect was. I got up to find out and saw a group of three boys not far away. They saw me at the same instant. They laughed when one of them said something I couldn't quite hear, and then they started toward me.

It didn't seem like a good situation and I started to run. But I twisted my ankle and fell, and before I could get up again, they were surrounding me. I noticed with surprise that one of them was Billy Croucher. "Hi, Billy," I said. He didn't answer. He fiddled with his belt loop and looked away from me. The biggest boy wore a leather wrist band with studs on it. He was sweaty—I could see beads of moisture over his lip. "You know her?" he asked Billy. Billy looked at me, and then at him.

"No," he said. "I don't know her." I thought that none of the boys could be very much older than I was, but there were three of them, and apparently they were together against me. I thought of the grasshopper I'd so recently held in my hands.

The biggest boy spoke. "Okay, take 'em off."

"Take what off?" I was still on the ground and I wondered if I should get up.

"Your pants!" he said, and the boys behind him snickered and moved restlessly.

I looked at them one at a time. When I came to Billy, he looked straight at me, and I saw nothing in his face that would help me at all. My throat began to hurt. "No," I said quietly.

"What?" the boy asked.

"No."

There was a pause, and I knew that he was deciding what to do. In that moment, I remembered something.

A huge dog once nearly bit me in the face, and I'd known the precise moment when he decided to do it. I'd been lying beside him watching him pant, mesmerized by the constant forward and backward motion of his black, sawtooth lips and his seemingly endless production of saliva. He looked at me in a rather friendly, investigative way. But then something crossed his eyes and I saw it; and I moved away just as he growled and lunged forward. I remembered that moment, and I understood that the time to do something was now.

"I live right up there," I said, pointing to the house nearest the gully.

The ringleader lifted his head and stared up to where I was pointing. "So?" He kicked me softly in the leg.

"So I can yell just one word, and my father will be right down here. He's home, and he was a German Nazi."

No one moved.

"I swear to God," I said. "One yell, and that's *it.*"

The ringleader looked at his friends. Then he turned fiercely back to me. "Okay," he said, in a low voice. "But don't you ever come back here again!"

I rose up. My ankle hurt badly, and I couldn't help limping, but I tried to make my back look proud and strong as I walked away. "Don't you ever come back!" the ringleader called.

I was almost to the top of the gully and I chanced turning around to look at the three of them. "I'll come back anytime I want," I said. *"Du bist ein schwein,"* I added. Anna had not reciprocated in vain. *"Schwein!"* I yelled, and then I burst into tears and ran as best I could toward home. They didn't win, I kept telling myself. They didn't get your pants off. But that seemed not to matter.

I missed Anna's lesson that afternoon. I stayed inside. I watched *My Little Margie* and read some fairy tales. I looked at spit under my microscope. Sometime near the end of the afternoon, though, I began to feel bad about not showing up, and I went over to her back porch. She was there, but she was with someone. I got closer and saw that it was Artie. I ran home, went up into my room, lay on the bed, and wept. It hadn't been a good idea, my matchmaking. I wished I'd never started it. It was dangerous. I went to my window and pressed my mouth to the screen. "Anna!" I yelled.

My mother came into my room with a basket of clean laundry. "What are you doing?" she asked. I turned around guiltily.

"Nothing."

She put some underwear in my drawer. "Aren't you going to help Anna today?"

"No," I said. "She's busy."

My mother looked closely at me. "Are you all right?"

"Yes." I felt stiff all over. Even my tongue felt stiff.

"Okay," she said doubtfully, and left. I stood at the window and stared over toward Anna's house, but all I could see was the roof. My heart hung huge inside me.

A week or so later, I read in my microscope use and care booklet that pond water was interesting to view. I took an empty jelly jar from the cupboard and went to the gully. I stood at the edge, looking to see if anyone else was there. I saw a monarch butterfly and ached to follow him, but it wasn't safe yet. I waited. After a long time, I ran quickly to the stream and filled the jar. I noticed the tepee was in ill repair, and I wanted to fix it. Instead, I ran home.

After I prepared the slide, I pulled my chair up to the microscope and focused it. I was astounded. Living in the water that I had imagined was crystal clear were forms of life that were disgusting to behold. It came to me that there was no place on earth that was pure. No person, either. In all of us was this mix of things, and the trick was to focus on the better parts. I could feel hope run free in me again, like unblocked circulation.

Carol Conroy returned the next day. I told her about Anna, and I told her about the incident in the gully. "I don't think we should go there anymore," I said. "We'll find another place."

"Well, *I'm* going," she said. "I'm going right now. Come on!"

I followed her reluctantly. "What if they come back?"

"They're only stupid *boys*. I know a curse my mother taught me that could rub them all out." I followed Carol down the familiar grassy hill to our tepee, which we spent the afternoon fortifying.

I resumed teaching Anna in the afternoons. I brought over my mother's wedding album and began with "bride" and "groom." Though Anna covered her mouth and giggled when she understood what the words meant, she repeated them right back to me. Earnestly. Flawlessly.

One Time at Christmas, in My Sister's Bathroom

It is 3:17 A.M. I am lying in bed looking at the dim outline of packed suitcases lined up neatly against the wall. My husband is snoring. I tap him gently. "Hey, Sam," I say. Nothing. I shake him.

"Yeah," he says. Then he begins snoring again. I turn on the bedside light. He squints, holds his arm up over his eyes. "What's the matter? What happened?"

"Nothing," I say. "I just . . . I don't think we should go."

He sighs deeply. "We already have tickets. It's tomorrow. We can't change our minds now—we'll lose a lot of money!"

I sit up and push my pillows behind me. Sam looks at the clock and winces. "Well, I'm sorry," I say. "But I can't sleep. I have to talk about this. You get married so if you can't sleep you can talk to someone."

He stares at me with red-rimmed eyes. "Where was that in the vows? If I'd known that, I'd have married JoAnn Anderson. She slept like a log. And when she got anxious, she painted her kitchen."

"Sam, listen. I'm serious. I know we'll lose money, but I don't want to go. I want to stay home for Christmas. Why can't we stay home for Christmas?"

"Because you told your parents we'd go there. And because we always go there."

"Well, not this year."

"Why not?"

"Oh, come on. What do we talk about every time we come home from there?"

"We decided the *kids* had fun. Remember?"

"Well, I know, but I just decided I don't want to do it anymore. I don't want to spend another Christmas worrying about my father's mood, tiptoeing around him, seeing him glower if something's not just right, listening to him order my mother around—"

"Kate."

"What?"

"This is old stuff. Your father's not going to change."

"Well, that doesn't mean I have to endure his behavior."

"The kids like to go to your parents'. It's the only time they get to visit them. Your mother would really be disappointed, too."

"Well, we're not going."

Sam reaches over to turn out the light. "Fine, we won't go."

I lie still for a while in the dark. Then I say, "All right, fine— we'll go."

As we begin our final descent, our son throws up. This is usual. I don't mind it, except for the part when I have to give the bag to the flight attendant, who acts not kind and professional, but personally offended. I want to say, "Look, he's a seven-year-old-kid who's embarrassed enough already. Don't make him feel worse." Instead, I always apologize.

This flight attendant, a young blond woman with a perfect hairdo, holds the bag away from herself between two perfectly manicured fingers. I clench my teeth. Then, "Sorry," I mutter. She shrugs, attempts a smile that fails, and then walks quickly down the aisle. I put my arm around Josh. "Don't worry about it," I say. "It's her job."

Josh's color is improving. "You always say that," he says.

"Do you feel all right now?"

"Yeah. Did I get any on you?"

"Don't worry about it." Mom will be thrilled, I think. She loves to do laundry. She's the only woman I know who really gets a bang out of transforming someone's dirty clothes into a perfectly folded, sweet-smelling pile.

I hear my daughter, Annie, twelve, asking Sam if Josh has to *always* throw up. She has tried to be quiet, but of course Josh hears her. "Shut up!" he hisses violently.

I sigh, look away from them. I hope they don't fight at my parents' house. My mother tries in vain to calm the situation while my father stares at the kids with a look on his face like he has just eaten something bad.

After we get our luggage, we see my parents waiting for us in the car outside. My mother is smiling and waving. As the kids run toward the car, I turn to Sam. "Here goes," I say grimly.

"You have a really terrible attitude," he says. Then he yells, "Mary! Frank! How are you?" and pulls me toward the car.

I climb into the backseat with the kids, smile hello. Maybe this time will be good, I think. My mother is so happy to see us. The food is always fantastic. I'm anxious to see my sister. I want to see if my brother-in-law likes this year's joke present, red lace boxer shorts.

When we arrive at the house, the kids go on their usual tour. My mother decorates everything—every single room in the house. Even the bathroom has holly wrapped around the shower rod, and a bath mat featuring a well-worn but eternally effervescent Santa Claus.

My father, Sam, and I sit at the kitchen table. I pour coffee for all of us. "Get me some cream, Kate, huh?" my father says. I feel myself stiffen. "Sure," I say. Maybe you'd like me to pour it in and stir it, too, I think. Then I decide that Sam is right—I do have a bad attitude.

"So how's the weather back home?" my father asks.

Sam shakes his head. "You know California—same thing every day. Nothing like Nebraska."

My father raises his eyebrow defensively. "No, we like seasons here."

Is this an argument already? I think. But if it is, Sam doesn't take the bait. "Yeah, sometimes I really miss the seasons. It's nice to have a white Christmas, that's for sure."

"Even if the windchill factor is ninety below zero," I say, and feel Sam kick me under the table. My father looks at me. "It is thirty-two," he says. "Above."

My mother comes in the kitchen. "More coffee?" she asks. My father holds up his cup, not looking at her, and she fills it.

"Sit down, Mom," I say. "You have some."

"Oh, I'm fine," she says. "How was the flight?"

"Well, Josh threw up," I say.

"Yes, I just helped him change," my mother says. "As soon as the load that's in there now is done, I'll wash his clothes."

"I'll do it," I say. "I need to do my blouse, too."

"Oh, that old washer is pretty temperamental," she says. "And

I'm going to be doing another load anyway." I had forgotten how much my mother is like a jealous lover when it comes to her washing machine.

I go upstairs to change, and then bring my blouse into the laundry room. My mother is there folding clothes, and holds out her hand to take my soiled blouse. "He still gets sick, huh?"

"Every time," I say. "Just as we land."

"He'll outgrow it," she says.

"When?"

"Soon, and then you know what?"

"What?"

"You'll miss it."

I smile. She's probably right.

She starts the washer and continues folding. I sort the socks. "You used to throw up in the car all the time," she says.

"I remember."

"And you outgrew it."

"Yeah—when I was twenty."

"Well, there you are. Only thirteen more years."

"You're such an optimist, Mom. Don't you ever look on the dark side?"

She looks at me. "What good would that do?"

I throw the socks I've folded into the basket. "I don't know. No good, I guess. I just wonder how you do it sometimes, that's all."

"Do what?"

I smile. "Nothing."

When I come upstairs, I see Sam in the living room, watching the kids look for their presents under the huge tree. I hear Josh say, "Here's one for Mom."

"Where?" I say, and go to look at it. It is a blouse-size box, and I decide that a blouse is what's in there. A blouse that says "nice girl" all over it, and that I will never wear. I am beginning to irritate myself. Why am I so nervous? I think, but I know why. I am nervous because I am waiting for something bad to happen.

Christmas Eve. Dinner is at my sister Jen's house. She has, as usual, knocked herself out: There is prime rib, but in case you don't like prime rib there is a ham. There are mashed white potatoes, but if you don't like those there are baked sweet potatoes. There are four different vegetables, canned and fresh. There are whole wheat and white dinner rolls. There are three kinds of pie: pecan, apple, and blueberry. "Only pie for dessert?" I ask.

"I've got an ice cream cake in the freezer," she says.

"Oh," I say. She doesn't know I'm kidding. I want to grab hold of her busy hands, say, "Oh, Jen, why do you do so much, try so hard? Are we all of us still afraid of him, still trying to do one thing that's right enough to win something from him?" But I don't say anything. I put on one of her aprons and ask what I can do to help. "You can finish stuffing the celery with cream cheese for the relish platter," she says. "And then would you put it out on the table? The kids are starving."

When I put the platter down between the candles on the dining room table, it is descended upon by Annie and Josh and their cousins, Jen's fourteen-year-olds, John and Lisa. They argue happily in their competition until my father asks loudly, "Can't you take *turns?* Don't any of you have any manners?"

All four of them stop, frozen. Then Josh puts back the celery stalks he had in his hand. "You can have them, Josh," I say.

"That's all right." He walks away into the kitchen. The other kids wait quietly, until one decides to go first. Then the others pick up black olives. One each.

My father switches channels on the television set, and settles into the recliner. I come into the living room and sit on the sofa. "How's it been at work?" I ask. "Busy?"

He nods, says, "Yeah," but doesn't turn his head from the screen. He is watching a variety show where the hostess, in a red, glittery gown, is singing "I'll Be Home for Christmas." I want Sam to be beside me, hearing this. I want him to get up and say, "Well, you're absolutely right, Kate. We could have had new kitchen cupboards for what we spent to come here." But Sam and my brother-in-law are busy in the basement trying to fix a snowmobile. They are drinking beer and laughing—occasionally the sound reaches upstairs, and everyone smiles. Well, almost everyone.

I go into the kitchen. Jen is making gravy. My mother is sitting at the table with a cup of coffee, while Josh leans companionably against her. "I got a phone call the other day, Josh," my mother is saying. "It was a big company in New York City, taking a survey." He smiles, looking down. He knows what's coming. "Guess what they wanted to know?" she says.

Josh's voice is very low. "Who the best seven-year-old in the world is."

My mother feigns great surprise. "Why, yes! That's it! And guess who I told them?"

"Josh Perkins."

"Right again!" She kisses him. He flushes and pulls away from her. "I gotta go see what John's doing."

My mother sighs, watching him walk away. "They grow up in one second flat," she says.

I sit down at the table with her. "Does Dad have to watch TV?"

I ask her. "Does he always have to watch TV? Last year he had it on when we were opening presents!"

"Oh, well, he doesn't really watch it," my mother says. "It's just for the companionship."

"Why doesn't he talk to his grandchildren for companionship?"

She toys with the handle on her coffee cup. "He's not too comfortable with conversation. Never has been. You know that, Kate."

Jen and I look at each other. "Let's turn it off," I say. "Let's just go in and turn it off and ask him who he thinks will win the Super Bowl this year. What he thinks of the president's foreign policy. If he likes the card Annie sent him—which, by the way, she spent two goddamn hours making!" No one speaks. I turn away to stir the gravy, which my sister has abandoned. "This is going to burn, Jen," I say.

"He can't be something different than what he is to please you, Kate," my mother says. "You should try to look at his good qualities once in a while."

I turn around. "You make it so easy for him, Mom! You always have! But you don't do any favors for anyone when you do that!"

She looks at me with a pained expression. "Don't, Kate. He'll hear you. It's Christmas Eve."

"I know," I said. "You can tell. The TV announcer keeps saying so." Jen leans hard against me. She's right. There's no point in this. "Oh, never mind," I say. "I'm sorry."

I go into the living room to see what the kids are doing. Lisa is pulling out a battered red leather scrapbook from the bottom shelf of the bookcase. I recognize it as being my sister's, from long ago. "This one's great," Lisa says. "This is from way before I was born, when Aunt Kate and Mom were little." My father, I notice, has turned his head from a cereal commercial toward us. "Want to see?" I ask. He shrugs. I walk over to the TV and snap it off. He takes in a breath, starts to protest, but then walks over to the sofa and sits down heavily.

I sit down beside him and we all begin looking at the black-and-white photos, held valiantly in place by a few remaining corner stickers. Lisa is narrator. "Here's when Aunt Kate was a baby," she says, and points to a picture of Jen as a five-year-old feeding me in a high chair. I am wearing a T-shirt and a diaper and Jen is in full cowgirl regalia. "Here's the dog they had in the olden days," she continues, and points to a sad-eyed boxer.

"Schatzi," my father says.

"Pardon?" I ask.

"Schatzi," he says again. "That was her name."

"Oh yeah," I say. And as I remember the dog's name, I remember the house where we lived with her, and the smell of my room, and the off-limits paraphernalia on Jen's dresser top, and my mother's hairdo and sweater sets and her youth. And I also remember my father: lean and handsome and scary. If he told you to do something and you did it instantly, you were safe. If you said, "Just a second," you were not. "He's *mean*," my friends would say, wide eyed, and I would look down and say, "I know."

Lisa is looking at a photograph of my mother with her mother. "Where's your mother in here?" Josh asks my father.

He pauses, then says, "She died when I was three."

"She did?" Josh swallows, stares at him, then at me.

"But she was very sick," I tell him. "She had a disease they couldn't cure then. But they can now."

"Oh," he says. Then he looks at my father and asks, "Did you cry when she died?"

It is so quiet in the room. Now, I am thinking. Now.

Then, "Dinner!" Jen calls and my father rises quickly and leaves the room. I start to follow him, but then detour to the bathroom, where I stand in front of the mirror and look at myself. And then I start to cry. I sit down on the edge of the bathtub and hold a towel to my face and cry with muffled gulps and I'm not even sure what it is I'm crying about. I hear a knock at the door, and stop crying. I splash cold water on my face and open the door.

"Are you all right?" Jen asks.

I nod. "My contact screwed up."

She smiles. "I don't think so."

I sigh, and sit back down on the bathtub. "Oh Jen, I don't know what I always expect. Maybe I'm a victim of too many *Father Knows Bests*. But I just wish . . . I don't know."

"Well, *I* know. But there's no point in asking people over and over for the impossible. He wasn't perfect, Kate. But he cares."

"You sound like Mom! How do you know he cares? Where's the evidence?"

Jen sits down beside me. "It's not so obvious. I mean, he didn't come home every night and give us little toys and tell us we were wonderful."

"That's for sure!"

"But he can't, Kate."

"Well, that's not okay with me. I hate how he treats Mom. I hate how he treats my kids—and yours. I won't let him do to them what he did to us."

She looks at me. "What did he do to us?"

I snort. "Come on!"

"No, what did he do?"

"Well, how's your self-confidence, for one thing? How long does it take you to trust men?"

Jen folds her apron in on itself. "You know, I'm a little tired of the old blame-your-parents routine."

I look away, don't say anything for a while. Then I say, "How hard would it be for him to act glad to see me when I come once a year?"

"That's a good question," Jen says. "Why don't you think about the answer?" She gets up and goes out the door.

I straighten the towels on the rack. I hear a knock and say nothing. Then the door opens and my father is standing before me. "You planning on eating sometime tonight?" He is still so tall, his voice so deep.

"Yes."

"Well, it's getting cold."

"I'll be right there." But I don't move.

"What's eating you anyway, Kate?"

I look up at him and wait for a long moment. Then I say, "All my life, I have been afraid of you." He blinks, says nothing. "All my life, I have waited for some moment of tenderness from you. And I don't remember a single one." He turns around and walks away, closing the door softly behind him.

I hear the clatter of silverware against plates, voices asking for the rolls to get passed. I should go out there, I think.

After a while, I hear another knock. This time it's Sam. When I see him, I fall against him. "Hey," he says. "What's going on in here?"

"I don't know, I don't know. I wanted things to be different this year. I always want things to be different. And they never are."

"What were you looking for?" he asks. "What did you expect?"

"I expected exactly what I got," I say, and I can taste how I feel. "But I was looking for . . . I was looking for him to say he can't *stand* how proud he is of me! That he held me as a baby and nearly burst inside! That he knows who I am, and he's glad about it!"

"And he has never done that."

"No!"

"And Kate, he never will." I start to cry again, and he sits on the toilet seat and pulls me onto his lap. He wipes my face off with toilet paper. He holds it up to my nose and says, "Blow," and I start to laugh. "Do you know who Clyde Tombaugh is?" he asks and I shake my head no. "He's the guy who discovered Pluto. He discovered Pluto, and then he walked down the hall to tell his boss, and then went to the movies. *The Virginian.* Gary Cooper."

"And?" I say.

"And nothing. That's all."

I *tsk,* get up off his lap. "Why did you tell me that? What's your point?"

He gets up and looks at himself in the mirror, plays with his hair a bit. "My point," he says, turning around to face me, "is that it seems we all of us return to what's familiar to us, no matter what. Even if it's not so wonderful, it's what we know. And it . . . I don't know, it sustains us." He puffs up his cheeks with air, lets it out, shrugs, and says, "See you in there. Better hurry up or all the gravy will be gone. And God, it's good."

He closes the door behind him. I sit down on the floor, my back against the wall. I am remembering a Christmas that was bitter cold, when my father took me with him to feed the ducks. He does this every Christmas Day, brings a sack of cracked corn to the lake and feeds the ducks. I don't know why I came that year; no one ever went with him. I was six. I sat in the car with the heater on and watched. I remember asking if the ducks' feet hurt—no boots; such cold, blue ice; such deep snow. My father said no, they were used to it. And then he stood at the edge of the water, throwing out handfuls of corn. There was one duck, a female, who hung back from the others, and as a result got no food. There was something the matter with her—one wing lay at an odd angle against her. My father kept trying to reach her, but she wouldn't come close enough to get anything. He edged out carefully onto the lake. I saw his breath as he spoke to her. Suddenly, his foot went through the ice. The water was deep enough to soak a good ways up his leg. He looked down, then simply crashed through with the other foot. Then he leaned over to dump the rest of the bag before the duck, who finally got some corn. When he got back in the car, I stared at his legs for a while. Then I said, "You got all wet." He shrugged, stared straight ahead. "Are you cold?" I asked.

"No," he said, though clearly he was. He backed the car up and started for home. "Your mother will have dinner ready by now," he said. "I want you to wash up as soon as we get in."

I open the bathroom door and go out to the table. "Rats! I guess this means I can't have your pie," Annie says.

"Hey, Mom, did you fall in?" Josh asks. "We thought you were a goner!"

"No," I say. "I had to do some things." I sit at the chair that has been left empty, next to my father. I see his arm moving, see him passing the rolls toward me. I understand that he is made up of working cells, just like me—crowded and confused pieces of genius that have been tampered with and now, wounded, go along in the way that they are able. I move a little closer to him. "Pass the gravy, please," I say.

He hands it to me. "Here. Merry Christmas."

"Merry Christmas," I say back, and I mean it.

Regrets Only

I was in the middle of making dinner when Laurence called. He told me he wanted me to meet his mother, who was in the hospital. Laurence is gay, his mother had a stroke, and he naturally assumed the two were inexorably linked. He wanted to pretend he'd had a major catharsis and was going straight. He said he was sorry he'd ever come out to her. It didn't work. It only broke her heart. And now look, he said, now she's had a stroke and maybe she'll die. "And she's just—well, she's so nice," he said. "I never told you much about her. She's so innocent! Like once we were watching a thing on TV about crack addicts and she got really sad and said, 'Why don't they just go get an ice cream soda? What do they need with all this stuff?' She was serious! Oh, I don't know, she's batty, I guess. But she's so *sweet!*" He was nearly hysterical and I was trying to get the lasagna in the oven.

"Can I call you back?" I asked. "I need to grate the Parmesan. If I do it on the phone everything gets too shaky."

"Just say yes," he said. "Say you'll meet her and tell her you're my girlfriend."

"Your girlfriend! I am a married woman—with a child. She'll see that right away."

"Well, for God's sake, don't wear your ring!"

"Listen, Laurence. A woman can just tell if another woman has children. You get these changes. It's like you can't make good gravy until you have children, and then suddenly you can."

"I can make good gravy," Laurence said, defensively.

"Not mother kind," I said. "You make fancy wine kind. You can't make mother kind. Anyway, what I mean is that your mother will sense right away that I have a kid, and then she'll know you're lying."

"Just because you have a child doesn't mean I'm lying! Why can't you be a single-mother girlfriend?"

"And what happened to my husband?"

"I don't know. Left you for another man."

"I'm sure." I stretched out the phone cord to look at myself in the glass door of the oven.

"Oh, come on. Please do it?"

I stared at the cheese and the grater. I wanted to get going. "For God's sake, Laurence, don't be so guilty all the time. You didn't make your mother have a stroke! You came out to her over ten years ago! Why don't you just think about this some more? Believe me, it's not a good idea. Too Lucy-and-Ethel."

"I can't believe you're letting me down on this. I've got nobody else I can ask! Please do it."

I narrowed my eyes. "Did you dream that you should do this or something?"

"Yes! Well, sort of. A daydream."

"They don't count."

"I know. But I did have a night dream that I gave her a gift. And then she died. Peacefully." There was a pause and then he added desperately, "I'm her only child."

"Oh, all right!"

"Great! I'll be there at seven. Fifteen minutes, that's all we'll be there. I promise. Remember not to wear your ring."

After dinner, my daughter, who thought Laurence's idea was terrific, who was acting like I'd been chosen to be on television, wanted to help me pick out something to wear. She thought I should look sexy. But then, she was twelve and temporarily tasteless. "You don't wear something sexy to meet your boyfriend's mother," I told her. "Especially when she's in the hospital. Remember that when you start dating."

"Laurence is trying to convince her that he likes women, right?" Her excitement was barely containable. I thought, Why don't *you* pretend to be his girlfriend if you think this is such a swell idea?

"Right."

She blew a huge orange bubble and then popped it. "So you should look sexy."

This is really too adult for her, I thought. Why isn't she in her room making a doll walk around and talking for her? Why doesn't she color anymore? Still, maybe she was right. I called down for advice to my husband, who was sitting in his armchair sighing over the newspaper. "How do I look sexiest?" I asked.

"T-shirt, no bra—why?" he yelled. There was a moment of silence, and then he asked, "Is Lynie with you?"

"Yes," she yelled back, "and I heard you. 'T-shirt, no bra.' That's disgusting."

"Forget it," I said. "I can't wear a T-shirt anyway. Let's go for the nice girl look." I held up a pink dress with a tiny white collar. "How's this?"

"Where'd you get that?" she asked. "It's pretty."

"From Grandma. She always wants me to wear stuff like this." I looked at myself when I was dressed. Not too bad. Conservative, but not Republican. The image of a woman who might still pray. I realized suddenly how much I didn't want to do this. I sat on the bed, frowning. Lyn sat beside me.

"All ready?"

"I'm nervous."

"Why? Laurence is your best friend."

"I know, but I don't want to meet his stupid mother and pretend I'm his girlfriend. This is too much to ask!"

"What about that time he sat for me when you and Daddy went away for the whole weekend?"

"He's forgotten all about that."

"Well, he still did it."

A car outside honked three times. "There he is," I said. Lyn ran down to meet him. She was crazy about Laurence. He called himself her fairy godfather. When she was born, he'd visited me in the hospital and brought her a Judy Garland tape. She listened to it every night, lay in her crib wide eyed and content, sucking her thumb to "The Man That Got Away." Their tastes had been aligned ever since. Laurence took her to museums, to concerts, even out to dinner. He came into the living room and hugged her, then waved to John. "How's it going?" he asked in the huskier-than-usual voice he reserved for my husband and members of the police force.

"Okay, Laurence, and you?"

"Okay." This was the usual length and caliber of their conversations. They didn't understand each other, but they tolerated each other with an excruciating kind of courtesy. When Laurence came to a family dinner, everyone was exhausted after an hour.

"You look nice," I told him when we got into the car. He was wearing his gray linen blazer and an imported cotton striped shirt, open at his tanned neck.

He waved my compliment away. "I'm a nervous wreck. I just thought maybe she'd feel better if she believed I'd have five Catholic children after she died. That's how many she and my father figured they'd have. But then he went and died on her."

"What? I have to be Catholic, too?"

"No, just raise our five kids to be."

"What makes you think she's going to die, anyway?"

"I don't know. She looks bad. Got all this junk on her."

"That doesn't mean anything," I said. "They like to play with all their equipment."

"I don't think she's going to make it," he said. I looked over at his serious profile and didn't say anything. I thought, Maybe this *is* a good idea.

The hospital room was a private. There were bouquets lined up on the windowsill and two cards, both featuring monster-type nurses, taped to the wall. There was a commode in the corner, covered by a blanket that served only to accentuate its presence. Laurence's mother was sitting up in bed watching television. When she saw us, she gasped and shut it off.

Laurence hugged her and said, "Hi, Ma. Look who I brought to meet you."

"Hello, Mrs. Davis," I said, and shook her hand.

"Oh, please . . . *Maureen*." She gave me a discrete once-over. I actually felt myself holding in my stomach. "It is such a pleasure to meet you, Susan. Laurence told me he'd met a very nice woman. How many children do you have?"

I looked at Laurence triumphantly, then said, "One."

"Uh-huh. Boy?"

"No, a girl. Her name is Lyn—she's twelve."

She smiled, "So. Larry tells me you're getting married soon." She straightened the transparent green tubing delivering oxygen through her nose.

I stared at Laurence while I said, "Oh, did he tell you that?" He stared back, his eyes wide and pleading. "Well, yes . . . some happy day," I said.

"When?"

"When?" I laughed a little. "Well, you know . . . we're sort of in the planning phase."

She took my hand and patted it. Then she looked over at Laurence, who had found something mesmerizing out the window. She leaned toward me, whispered, "I knew he never meant it. I knew he only had to find the right girl." There was a small clicking sound when she talked—loose dentures, I imagined. She had nice eyes, blue and clear, and curly white hair. I thought she looked fine. I didn't see a thing wrong with her. Then I wondered if something were hidden by the covers and felt guilty. She was looking at me expectantly.

"Yes, we're . . . very happy. Very excited," I said.

"Larry is a wonderful boy."

"Yes, he is."

"Very sensitive."

"Oh, yes."

She sighed, let go of my hand. "Of course, I hate for you to meet me under circumstances such as these! When I get home, you must come to dinner."

"Well, I'd . . . love to."

She turned toward Laurence. "Will you bring her to dinner next weekend?"

He turned around, and there was, I noted with satisfaction, a residual blush on his face. "Ma, you don't know when you're going home."

"Sure I do. In two days."

"You're kidding."

"No, Dr. Abrahms told me today. It was a very small stroke, Larry—I'm fine. I was very lucky. I just have to take this medicine—to thin my blood, you know. I'm going home Friday."

"Well!" He looked at me. "Isn't that great news! I wasn't expecting that!"

She chuckled. "He always underestimates me. He worries too much. He's very sensitive."

"Oh, I know." I thought, I'm going to kill him.

"Ma, you must be tired. I just wanted you to meet Susan, say hello. We can talk more later."

She nodded. "Young lovers! You two go right ahead. I'm so glad to meet you, Susan." She looked at me significantly. "Me too," I said.

Laurence kissed her. We started to leave the room and she called me over and asked in a low, conspiratorial tone, "Do you like roast beef, honey?"

"Yes, I do," I said. "Roast beef is just fine." I was speaking in a low voice too, although I had no idea why.

"I could roast a chicken, too."

"Either one. But you go ahead and just rest, now."

"Larry *loves* apple pie," she whispered. "Do you?"

"Oh yes, who doesn't?" I raised my voice. "Well, it was very nice meeting you."

"Okay, dear. Before you go, hand me my phone, will you? I'm going to call my sister. Wait till she hears that I've just met my future daughter-in-law!" I handed her the phone and she waved gaily to me as we left.

In the hall, I squeezed Laurence's arm and said between my teeth, "I thought she was on her *death*bed!"

He whispered back, "Oh fine, wish my mother the worst!"

"You know what I mean! Now what? I'm not going to her house for roast beef and apple pie, I'll tell you that."

"*I* know!"

"Well, what are you going to say? That we broke up on the elevator?" As if on cue, the elevator arrived. We stepped in and I said, "I've had it. I want to break up. We're through."

The doors closed. Laurence stared straight ahead and said sadly, "Finished. And so soon!"

Back in the car, I punched him on the arm. "She's not even sick! She looks better than both of us."

He looked at himself in the rearview mirror. "Do I have those bags under my eyes?"

I imitated him in a nasty, whiny voice. "Do I have those bags under my eyes?"

"All right, I'm sorry!" he said. "She looked much worse yesterday!"

"Oh, never mind. I got to get out of the house, anyway. Let's go eat. Want some pie?"

"No."

"Okay, let's go get some."

"Okay."

At our favorite downtown diner after two slices each of banana cream, I said, "I can't believe she *bought* all that!"

"Oh, it's because she never believed me when I told her the truth. She's just been waiting for this. Now she's happy."

"But what about you? Look what you've done! She'll probably live to be a hundred and be asking you every day about your upcoming wedding. Why did you do this, Laurence, seriously? Did you really think she was going to die?"

He fingered his coffee cup. "I don't know, maybe."

"I think it was a subconscious desire on your part. I think you wanted to think about being married to me, 'cause for a woman, I'm pretty swell."

"Maybe you're right."

I stopped my cup at midpoint. "Really?"

"Maybe we should have an affair."

"Oh, stop."

"Maybe we should," he said. "Don't tell me you've never thought about it."

"Only when I first met you, five hundred years ago, and I didn't know you were gay." I remembered meeting Laurence for the first time in our acting class in college, admiring his wonderful looks, his sense of humor. He'd told me soon after that, "Look, I think I should tell you something. I'm not interested in women . . . that way."

"Well, *I* know!" I'd said. "I know that!" But I hadn't. And I was disappointed. I'd been thinking, Oh boy, a man with clean nails who loves theater and books, a man who's emotionally available. But then we became good friends and I thought, Well, this is better anyway. Now we won't get sick of each other. And we didn't.

"You've never thought of it since then?" he asked.

"No! Have you?"

"Oh, sometimes. Sometimes when things are going badly with someone, I think, Maybe it would be easier to be more of a majority type. You know, pull the Saab into the garage each night, hug the kids, eat supper, and watch television with the wife."

"God, you make it sound so boring."

"Well, isn't that pretty much what you do?"

"Yes. And it is boring. But it's nice, too. I don't know—sometimes you think you're going to scream with the sameness of it all, with the unending chorus, with having to see everyone at their worst, and vice versa. But you always have a date for the prom. You don't have to eat alone. And then every once in a while John will sort of collapse onto me and say how much he loves me and hold real still and I'll look out over the top of his head and think, Yes, well, this is all right. And I love Lyn so much! It's a different kind of dimension in love, kids. Sometimes I really feel sorry for you, that you won't ever know that kind of love. Do you feel bad about missing it?"

"I see Lyn a lot. She feels like my kid."

"No, it's different when they're really yours."

"That's what everybody says. I guess I am sorry I won't have that. But we all have major regrets about things we've missed. I'm sure you do too. Don't you?"

I thought for a while and then said, "I'm sorry I didn't take acid and explore the sewers with these friends of mine in college."

"Who, Ron *Shenk*man and those guys?"

"Yeah, they came to get me to go with them one night. They were these really huge pipes. They said it was . . . well, what they said was that it was far out. Remember? 'Far fuckin' out, man.' "

"I didn't like those guys."

"Oh, they were all right. They were fun!"

"Exploring the sewers on acid. Really a compelling idea. This is your major life regret."

"You had to know them. I did take acid with them once. It was at Ron's house. I really liked looking at his dog, at the plants in his house. They seemed filled with a kind of primordial knowledge; they seemed like *the answer.* I looked down into a flower on one plant, and it was so complex and beautiful and I kept saying, 'See? It's all right *here.*' And then I remember I went outside. It was really dark, and I wasn't afraid at all, which is really unusual for me. I looked up in the sky and all the stars seemed connected by these white lines, like constellation maps, and I thought, Aha, *that's* how those guys came up with those things! They ate some LSD and then forty-five minutes later, they were saying, 'Hey, look! Do you see a *winged horse* up there? How about a bull? Oh wow—he has a red eye! See that? Far fuckin' out, man! Psychedelic!"

Laurence smiled. "Where did twenty years go?"

"I don't know. Want to go?"

"Yeah. Let's leave the waitress a big tip. She had a hanky sticking out of her breast pocket."

We drove in silence for a while. Then Laurence said, "Well, what do we owe our parents? I just wanted the rest of my mother's life to be peaceful."

"Oh, maybe I *should* go to dinner with you, and be really obnoxious—talk with food in my mouth, bang on the table with my spoon while I make obscure political points—and then she'd be happy for you to get rid of me."

"That would only make you fit right in. She'd probably give you some of her best Tupperware at the end of the evening—a little starter set to officially welcome you into the family." He sighed, pulled the car over to the side of the road. "I'm depressed. I don't know what I'm doing."

I touched his arm. "Well . . . Laurence. What *is* it?"

He leaned back, stared at the ceiling. "I don't know! I feel like this voice is saying, 'Lauuurrrreeence! It's ten o'clllooooock. Do you know where you are?' Is this a midlife crisis?"

"I don't know. Maybe. Want to get out? Walk a little?"

"Sure." We went into the woods by the side of the road. Laurence looked over at me. "It's really dark out here. Are you scared?"

"Nah."

"I'm scared," he said.

"I know. I'll help you if I can."

"I don't know what I need."

I sat down on the low branch of a tree, and Laurence sat beside me. I said, "You know, I think when you face the prospect of losing a parent, all kinds of things get shaken up. Maybe you have to sort of redefine yourself, only this time on your own terms."

"I don't know. Maybe." He stood and looked down at me. "For a boring suburban housewife, you're pretty smart. And you are so beautiful. Still."

"*Laurence.*" I felt my heart rate quicken, and I found it profoundly confusing. I laughed, and it was too loud. Then I cleared my throat.

"You're nervous!"

"Well, yeah, aren't you?"

"Yes. Because I would like to kiss you."

"Laurence, I think you're taking this whole thing too seriously. I mean, you don't have to live up to your mother's expectations, even if she is dying. And by the way, she's not. She's getting ready to make a roast beef."

"I know. It's just that . . . I don't know . . ."

"Didn't you ever have a girlfriend?"

"No."

"So you never kissed a girl, even?"

"No."

I was incredulous. "Spin the *bottle*?"

"No!"

"Boy!"

He was irritated. "Well, did *you* ever kiss a girl?"

"Of course! How do you think we practiced for the real thing?"

"A real, sexual kiss?"

"Well, no. It was through a pillow."

"Right. That's not it, and you know it."

I picked up a blade of grass, began to peel thin, supple strips from it. "I'll kiss you if you want." He didn't answer. "Of course, you don't have to."

"No, it's . . . I do want to."

"Okay," I said. "Do you want to be serious? Should I do my best stuff?"

"Yes," he said, and I heard a slight tremor in his voice. "I want to be serious."

"Okay," I said, and closed my eyes.

"I mean it!" he said.

"Okay!" I closed my eyes again. My lids were jerking wildly.

He took his jacket off and spread it on the ground. "Lie down."

I opened my eyes. "Laurence! That's your four-hundred-dollar Italian blazer from Mr. Eric's!"

"You have to be lying down. We have to relax."

I shrugged. "Okay." I lay down and smoothed my skirt beneath me.

"You look nice in a dress. I hardly ever see you in a dress."

"Thank you."

"And . . . you smell nice, too."

I swallowed, and watched as he lay down next to me. He turned on his side, put one hand along the side of my face, pushed his fingers into my hair, and kissed me. His lips were slightly rough, but nice. He was a very sensual kisser. I felt my stomach start to soften, and I kissed him back. It was a long kiss, deep, and when he pulled away I was breathless and full of desire. I thought, Oh, I've been married so long. We're in a kind of rut. Affairs can actually make marriages better. He's such a good friend, he's so handsome. I'll do it. I looked over at him. He was on his back, looking up into the sky. "Are you okay?" I hoped he would rise up and kiss me again soon.

"Yes," he said. "I'm okay. God, I didn't feel anything." I was quiet, and he turned his head to look at me. "I mean, *nothing!*"

"Fine!" I said. "I *heard* you!"

"Oh." He touched my arm. "I'm . . . sorry."

"It's okay." I sat up. "So. So much for thinking maybe you'd make a major change for real. Of course, maybe I'm just not your type."

He put his hand on my back. "No, if I went for women, you'd be the one."

I looked at my watch. "I'd better go home. I need to help Lyn with some French."

"Her teacher's an asshole, you know."

"Her French teacher?"

"Yes. Did she tell you what he did to the kid who forgot his homework twice in a row?"

"No, what?"

"He had to stand at the blackboard with his nose in a circle. It was high up—the kid had to stand on his tiptoes."

"Jesus!"

"She didn't tell you?"

"No. She tells you everything. I just clean her room."

We walked back to the car. Laurence turned on the radio, then turned the volume down low. "Do I need to say I'm sorry again?"

"I don't think so. No, you don't need to apologize."

"I'm sorry, Susan."

"Okay."

"*Do* you think you should come to my mother's house for dinner?"

"No!"

"You're right, this was a stupid idea. But I can undo it all gradually."

"Yeah, don't tell her the truth all at once. It can be hard to take."

"I know." He reached for my hand.

He drove me home and I told him to go slowly down the neighborhood streets so I could look inside all the houses we passed. I liked seeing people being themselves, walking around in T-shirts or robes, eating something they held in their hands. I liked seeing what was up on all the walls, especially if I hated it. "Look at that *painting* over that couch!" I told Laurence as we passed one ranch-style house.

"Oh, Jesus, look at the *couch!*" he said.

"I can't believe some people," I said. "I can't believe what some people like."

He drove even slower. He drove so slowly I thought maybe we'd get pulled over for looking suspicious. But we needed to do this. We needed to make sure we weren't missing anything.

The Thief

Kate Conway groaned so loudly in aisle three of the Shop 'n Save that people around her stood still for a moment, waiting to see what would happen next. But nothing happened next. Kate was simply reading the ingredients list on a box of Frosted Fruity O's, and when she finished she simply put the cereal in her basket. She had promised her children the night before that she would buy it for them today. "We never get to eat anything fun," they had complained. "It won't kill us, you know!" Kate had her doubts about that, but David had sided with them, saying, "Look, it's fine that you're so conscientious. I want them to be healthy, too. But if you go too crazy, they'll only rebel later on. They'll be perpetual graduate students living in infested walk-ups, subsisting on nitrates and dye just to spite you."

After she checked out, she wheeled the basket of groceries toward her van, thinking, Why do I get so obsessed about things like nutrition anyway? It's because I'm bored. It's because my life has become flat. I wish I was having an affair with the butcher. She raised the hatch and loaded the bags in, envisioning the man at the meat counter. He was very handsome. She imagined him looking at her as though she were beautiful. Nah, she thought, slamming the door shut. We'd only break up, and then I'd be embarrassed to ring the bell and ask for better-looking rib roast.

She started the van and turned the radio on. At first, when she heard two voices, she thought the station wasn't tuned in properly and she reached for the dial. Then she realized a man's voice was coming from behind her seat. "A beautiful day in Boston!" the radio said. "Go straight home," the other voice said.

This is a joke, she thought. She started to turn around and the voice said, *"Don't."* Oh, she thought. I see. This is not a joke. It is something else.

"I know where you live," the voice said. "Don't think about going anywhere else." She swallowed, put the car in gear, and started toward the exit of the parking lot. Her arms felt curiously heavy. This is Thursday, at one o'clock, she thought. The sun is out. People are going into the store with coupons. I don't have to do this. All I have to do is tell someone, get some help. She saw a man walking nearby, and put her foot on the brake, slowing the car. Then she felt something cold and hard being pushed into her ribs, and the voice said, "I said don't try anything, remember?"

"Okay," she said. "I'm not." She emptied her mind of everything, and drove the six blocks home. When she pulled into her driveway she looked for a neighbor, but saw no one. She got out of the car and watched as the man followed her. He looked around quickly, then flashed her the gun hidden under his jacket. It was black. Funny, Kate thought. I thought guns were silver, like Pete's cowboy gun. I thought they were silver and kept in jeweled holsters, and would never be serious. She was aware of a vague pain in her stomach, but it seemed to belong to someone else. She felt suspended above herself, a reluctant viewer of her own life.

"Get your groceries and get inside," the man said. He was young—maybe twenty-five—and good-looking, someone you'd be tempted to pick up hitchhiking. His eyes were light blue, clear, and looked directly at her.

"My groceries?" she asked.

"Yeah, you just got groceries, right?"

"Yes, but . . . never mind them."

The man gestured angrily with the lump in his jacket. "Get them! Why should you let food spoil?"

She got the bags and went into the house. The man closed, then chain-locked the front door. She set the bags on the kitchen table and turned to face him. She had begun to cry.

"What's the matter?" He seemed genuinely surprised.

"I'm *afraid*, that's what!"

"I'm not going to hurt you, okay? This is just a robbery."

She frowned. "You're going to *rob* me?"

"Yeah."

"Well, why didn't you come when I wasn't home?"

"Because I don't know where anything is." She stared at him. "Put your frozen things away before they melt."

She started to laugh, but then reached for one of the bags. She pulled the box of cereal out and put it on the table. The man picked it up. "You feed your children this shit?"

"Not usually." She put away the frozen foods resentfully. She didn't want him to see what else she'd bought. When she was finished, he said, "All right, let's take a little tour."

They began upstairs. He went into her son's room and looked around. "Who's room is this?"

"My son's."

"What's his name?"

"Bobby," she lied.

"How old is he?"

"Eleven." She walked over to his bed, straightened the corner of the spread.

"Anything valuable in here?"

She looked at Pete's Yankees cap, at the postcards on his bulletin board. And then she saw him sitting at his school desk, his hand that was not done growing holding his pencil, and was suddenly furious. "Well, of *course* there are valuable things in here. Everything is valuable in here! But not to you! You don't need anything in here! If you want something, take my jewelry!"

The man sighed. "Look at this. You see? You have no self-worth. You just go right ahead and tell me to take *your* things." He shook his head. "This is a real problem for women."

He's crazy, she thought. He's crazy and he has a gun. "I'm sorry," she said. "I'm a mother. It's just a mother thing, you know; it's instinctive to protect your children."

"Yeah," he said. "My mother, I don't think she had that thing." He pulled open the top dresser drawer. "Seriously, does he have anything valuable?"

She thought for a moment. "No."

He looked at her. "If I find something, you'll be real sorry."

"There's nothing! Well, he has a coin collection, all right?"

"Is it worth anything?"

"Just a couple hundred dollars."

The man raised his eyebrows. "Just a couple hundred dollars, huh?" She looked away from him. "Where is it?"

She got the coin collection from the top shelf of the closet and held it out toward him. "Put it in a pillowcase for me," he said. She went to the linen closet and dug through the pile of pillowcases.

She'd give him an ugly one. She found a floral pattern she'd never liked, put the coin collection in it, and gave it to him. He pulled some black gloves out of his jacket and put them on.

She would be very cooperative, she decided. She wouldn't offend him. She'd be wooden; she'd get through this. Tonight, she would be in the bathtub, fine, she knew it. The children, unaware of the day's events, would be in their beds with the clean sheets she'd put on that morning, pink-cheeked and sound asleep. David would be sitting on the lid of the toilet, leaning earnestly toward her, listening to her tell about this very moment. She would have a washcloth lying warm over her chest. David would be very concerned and loving. "Would you like some wine?" he would ask. "Some cocoa? Oh, my poor, brave darling." The thief would be in jail being eyed by vicious psychopaths twice his size. She felt light-headed and leaned against the door frame. "What's wrong?" the man asked.

"I think I feel a little faint."

"Sit down!" he said. "And put your head between your knees."

Her throat tightened as she slid down onto the floor. "Are you going to shoot me?"

He *tsked*. "Didn't I say I wasn't going to hurt you? What kind of person do you think I am?"

She pressed her knees into her eyes. In a moment, she felt stronger, and stood up. She looked into the man's face. "Why are you doing this? Don't you know you can ruin your whole *life* doing this?" He didn't move. She sighed, then asked, "Have you ever done this before?"

"No." His face was full of pain. He was so young. She saw his heart beating in the hollow of his neck. She wasn't afraid anymore. She was a little tired, in fact.

"Are you in some kind of trouble?" she asked.

His face changed. "Let's go." He pointed the gun at her. "Now. Show me something worth something."

"I'll show you my jewelry," she said. "You can have that. Really, that's the only thing that's worth much."

She took him to her bedroom and pointed to her jewelry box. While he went through it, she studied his clothes. She would need to remember them when she called the police. He'd probably be easy to catch even without the description. He was obviously inept, some scared kid acting out on a Thursday afternoon in suburbia. Still, she memorized his outfit. He was wearing gray corduroy pants and a black-and-white checked flannel shirt. No belt. Black high-top sneakers. He bought those clothes somewhere, went into a store and was seen as a regular customer. "Have a nice day," someone told him, and he probably said, "Same to you." Then he went home and put these clothes on and went out to rob people. She wondered where he lived. She wondered how he knew where she lived. The man held up her pearls, examined them in the light from the window, then threw them back in the box. "You're not taking those?" she asked. He shook his head no. She watched him for a while, putting her opal brooch, her diamond earrings into the pillowcase. He took her gold watch, her ruby ring, her antique emerald bracelet. Then he closed the box. "What's wrong with the pearls?" she asked.

"Not a good quality. Not worth much."

She flushed. "My husband gave me those pearls for my fortieth birthday! They happen to be very high quality!"

The man looked at her sympathetically. "Your husband is cheap," he said. "But look, if it'll make you feel better . . ." He opened the box and threw the pearls in the pillowcase. "There," he said. "Okay?"

She sniffed. She'd ask David about those pearls. For God's sake, it was for her fortieth! As the man closed the box again, he saw a corner of paper sticking out from behind the satin lining. He pulled it out. Kate reached for it. "That's nothing," she said. "That's just . . . personal."

"Well, let's see what you've got here. Let's see what's personal about you."

"Please," she said, but he had stepped back from her and was reading aloud from the slip of paper.

" 'Asparagus incident,' " he said. " 'Bad dream. Interruptions. No reception. Onus on me to always come up with ideas.' " He looked up, puzzled. "What the hell is this?" Kate looked out the window. "Hey!" he said loudly, and she jumped.

"It is my . . . divorce list," she said.

"Your what?"

"It is things I write down in case I ever decide to get a divorce. To justify it."

He looked at the paper. "The *'asparagus* incident'?"

"Yes, that's one."

"What happened?"

"Well, I certainly don't feel I need to tell you!"

"Oh, please . . . what's your name?"

"Jane," she said.

"Oh, please, Jane. *Jane!* Your name's not Jane! Nobody's name is Jane!"

"Well, mine is."

"So tell me about the asparagus, Jane." She was silent. "Tell me or I'll shoot a hole in your armoire."

"It's just to remind me of times when he overlooks my needs, okay? Like once I specifically asked him to save the leftover asparagus and he threw it out anyway!"

The man stared at her. "This is grounds for divorce? No wonder the country's going to hell in a handbasket!"

"No!" She cleared her throat, then lowered her voice. "It's just that I feel like my opinion doesn't count, that he always just goes ahead and does what he wants. The asparagus is a symbol."

"Well, that's inspired, Jane." He looked at the list again. "What about 'bad dream'? What happened there?"

She looked down, spoke quietly. "I had a bad dream, and I cried out in my sleep, and my husband woke up and told me, "Shhhh!" and went back to sleep."

"You're kidding!"

"No."

"You mean that's all? He didn't grab you and hold you, ask you what the matter was?"

"No."

"That is bad."

She took the list from him. "Please don't do this anymore. I find this very humiliating. And unnecessary."

"Okay."

"Do you want anything else?"

He didn't answer for a moment, looked as though he were confused. Then he said, "Yeah. Show me the other rooms." She took him to her daughter's room, with its teddy bears and Golden Books and pink plastic cup by the bedside, filled with last night's water. He picked up a picture frame, then put it back down. "Okay," he said. "Downstairs."

She showed him the dining room, David's study. He found

nothing he wanted. In the living room, he picked up a shell from the coffee table and put it in the pillowcase. "Why are you taking that?" she asked.

He shrugged. "I like it."

"Why don't you find your own damn shell?"

"I want what you picked."

"What makes you think I picked it?"

"Didn't you?" She was silent. She would never find another shell like that one.

The parakeet chirped from his cage in the corner and the man walked up to him, whistled softly, and said, "Hello, pretty boy." The bird fell silent, and Kate was happy. Later, she'd give him lettuce for that, teach him to say, "I'm a hero! I'm a hero!" "Neat!" her children would say. "Archie can say something new!"

When they went to the basement, the man saw a tiny safe built into the wall. "What's in there?"

"The truth is, I don't know," Kate said. "Nothing, I assume. It was put in by the people who lived here before us, and we've never been able to get it open."

He walked up closer to it. "This the combination on the index card here? Great idea, putting it right next to the safe."

She shrugged. "It doesn't work anyway. That's how it was when we moved here, and we've never changed it."

He tried the numbers. The safe stayed locked. He spun the dial around again, and the safe opened. "I don't believe it!" Kate said. "How'd you do that?"

"Backwards," the man said. He reached in and pulled out a blue velvet sack. "Well, look here!" He turned the bag upside down and a diamond necklace fell into his hand. It looked like ones Kate saw in magazines and thought no one could possibly own. "Jane," the man said sadly. "You lied to me."

"I swear I didn't!" Kate said. "We really could never open it! If I knew that necklace was there, would I leave the combination beside it?"

The man considered this as he moved the necklace about in his hand, watching it sparkle. "Absolutely dazzling, isn't it? It almost seems alive." He looked up at her. "Come here, Jane." She swallowed, stood her ground. "Come here!" he said, "or I'll goddamn shoot you, I don't care what I said!" She walked up to him slowly. He put his hands on her shoulders, kissed her forehead lightly, and then turned her around. He lay the necklace against her, then fastened it at the back. His fingers were so warm. She smelled soap. "Now: Happy Fortieth," he said. She stood still, not breathing, until he took his hands away and spoke again. "Is that all you have to show me?"

"Yes."

He turned her around and stared at her with a certain intimate weariness. "You sure?"

The necklace was cold against her neck. It was also surprisingly heavy. "Yes, I . . . I'm sure."

He sighed, looked around the room. "You got an awful lot of Barbie dolls down here, Jane."

"I know. My daughter likes them."

"You shouldn't buy her so much. You'll spoil her."

"I suppose."

"So don't you have any decent artwork? Some small oils?"

"No."

"I'm disappointed in your taste, Jane."

"My apologies."

They walked upstairs. He took an apple from her fruit bowl on the kitchen table. Then he went to the door, turned, and handed her the pillowcase. "I changed my mind," he said.

"What do you mean?"

"I just changed my mind. So how about you don't call the cops on me, all right, Jane?"

She folded the top of the pillowcase down on itself, over and over. There was a lot of room. He hadn't taken much. He was a terrible thief. "Yes, all right."

"Your neck is beautiful, Jane. Long, and elegant—like you came down from royalty or something."

"Thank you."

He showed her the gun again. "This can't hurt you, Jane. It's a starter's pistol. I used it for a race today."

"Oh. Well, it looks very real. Very convincing."

"Does it?"

"Yes."

"I really wish you wouldn't call the cops, Jane. I never did anything like this before. And I never will again. You know that, don't you?"

She looked down, didn't say anything. Then she said, "You didn't really know where I lived."

"Of course not. I just saw you go into the store, and got this . . . idea. I don't know. I'm sorry."

"What's your name?" she asked.

"My name's Jane, too."

"No, it isn't."

"You're right. It's Jonathan Hansen. I'm in the phone book— Girard Street. Look me up sometime, Jane. We'll have lunch." He smiled slightly, and left.

She chain-locked her door and watched him walk down the sidewalk. He was eating the apple. Then she went to the phone book. There it was, at the top of the column, in clear black print.

Jonathan, his mother had named him. And then what? Dreamlike, she dialed his number. A recording said, "Hello. I'm not here now. But please—leave a message." His voice was so familiar. She shivered, hung up, and dialed the police. Then she thought, no. It's not his voice that's familiar. It's the longing in it. She put her hand to the back of her neck, and followed the hard line of diamonds around to the base of her throat. When she heard the policeman identify himself, she hung up. She was quiet when she did it. She was absolutely noiseless.

Today's Special

I used to think that the best thing to do when you had the blues was to sit in a warm bathtub, almost too hot, and slouch down far enough that the water level was just below your chin. That way, you could feel protected by the depth, and cleaned in a deeper than usual way by the rising steam. The problem with that method is you had to keep fooling with the faucet to keep the temperature just right, and that would break the healing spell. Now I think it's better to go to a diner and eat a fried egg sandwich. You have to look around a bit to get the right diner and the right kind of sandwich. It's not as easy a combination to find as you might think. Diners have opted for a lot of illegitimate foods, abandoning things that are real (serving, for example, instant mashed potatoes instead of the familiar real potato lumps that make us crazy with desire and nostalgia—oh, you have to be careful and look hard). Anyway, what you do is you find a good diner, and when you have the blues, you go and eat there. You can't bring a journal, because then everybody notices you and they change what they do, assuming somehow that they are what you're writing about, and that therefore they need to do a little behavioral tie-straightening. So you leave your journal at home. It's good to bring a newspaper, though, so you can pretend you're really not much interested in anything going on around you. Then people really open up.

I had a friend once who was so filled with sadness it seemed to come pouring out of her at every opportunity. Say the event was no more than hearing about some animal dying, somebody's pet. She'd take information like that very seriously; and it was hard for her to be here. In spite of her own burden of pain, though, or perhaps because of it, she felt compelled to help others. She wanted a lighter load all around. And I wanted to help *her*. But I didn't know how. Now the diner seems to me to be the thing I might have presented her. For there we all are, confessing our need for complex carbohydrates, unabashedly feeling some improvement in our spirits (even if they weren't that bad) after some pancakes and syrup. *Real* pancakes with *real* syrup, I should say.

There's a diner three blocks from my house whose only serious errors are the wrong kind of dishware (too light) and the wrong kind of potatoes (instant). I asked the waitress there once why they didn't use real potatoes, since everything else was so legitimate. She looked up from her pad to ask me if I had ever peeled a whole sack of potatoes. I allowed as how I hadn't. "Well," she said, "there you are." She readjusted her pencil and her gum while I noticed with disappointment that she no longer wore her hair net either.

However, there are booths at the diner, and the necessary gold speckles in the Formica, which is only slightly yellowed, and then in only certain lights, like forty-year-old teeth. The booth seats are red leatherette, with just a couple of discrete tears, in only one bench. There's a counter, too, with stools that spin around completely when a kid's sitting on them, or turn only modestly with an adult's repressed mentality in charge. Salt and pepper are in glass containers as they ought to be. Sugar is in the tall holder with the trapdoor that lets you pour to your heart's content and doesn't make you feel guilty or wasteful the way opening more than one sugar packet might. Ketchup and mustard show up on your table when the waitress thinks it's appropriate for them to show up, which is almost always. You can get meat loaf, sliced exactly the right thickness, with brown gravy that really isn't from a can. You get peas and (instant) mashed potatoes and two slices of white bread with that. I get milk in a white-blue plastic glass, too. Most other adults I see there opt for the coffee, maintaining some secret tradition and addiction.

Well, you order whatever you want. It might be the meat loaf or it might be a Greek ensemble—a salad with feta cheese, lemon rice soup, baklava. It might be chicken croquettes with their suspicious yellow gravy. It doesn't matter too much—it's all fine. The point is that you don't see people there all dressed up and pulling out American Express Gold Cards. You see them in their natural states. Oh, there might be the secretaries all a little overdressed and poignantly hopeful, with their bangle bracelets and nail polish and perfect hosiery. They make out like this is strictly a temporary stop. But they give themselves away with what they order. We all do in the diner. "Give me some of that, uh, American chop suey," we say, meaning, "Take me home to an older kitchen, a less complicated time, a presence that offered silent acceptance." People talk in the most casual and unaffected of ways. We share the weather like a present marked "For all of you." "Isn't it *nice?*" we ask one another. Someone will almost always come through as a bit more knowledgeable than all the others, with a long-range fore-cast, and it's almost always someone who's been nursing a cup of coffee for a good forty minutes.

It makes me feel well cared for, this sharing of information. And I am captured by the more personal conversations because of their easy simplicity, their honesty. Gossip isn't sharp or malicious—it's necessary, human reporting, and we listen with ears far more sym-pathetic than critical.

And then, of course, it's the orderliness and the predictability that make me feel better too. There's a cop that's always at the diner around eleven. He eats an early lunch as counterpoint to my late breakfast. We never speak, but we know who the other is. I wouldn't mind if he did speak to me. For his part, he'd never give me a ticket.

I like the toned-down rattle of dishes, the way the world takes on a less hysterical cast and seems more washed and ironed. I even like the way people smoke here, though I am an adamant non-smoker in other situations. All I need to do is eat the meat loaf and to see that others do more or less the same, and I lose the blues. One, two, three.

So here is where I'd bring my friend, if I could reach her. "Look," I'd say. "Look around here and see: doesn't this show you that it's only the small things that we love the best, that make the real difference? Nothing big ever replaces the sight of the winter boots all lined up, or the sound of the click of the front doors locked against the darkness each night. Consider cooling pies. The impossibly small size of your own child's shoe. The briefest look in your direction from a particular set of eyes at the moment your heart needs it most. Isn't it those small things that add the necessary shape and meaning to our lives? And don't we miss seeing them if we look too hard for big things?" Oh, I'd bring her here if I could, all right, and order for her myself. Cheeseburger and a malted. Fries on the side. Coleslaw, and pie at the end. "I don't know what could possibly work any better than this," I'd tell her. "You try this, and see."

As it is, I go alone. I sit at a booth for four anyway, with my newspaper for company. Nobody there seems to make a thing of it. It's because somewhere under our breaths, we're all singing the same song. And although it's only us sharing the same notes in the same way, some ethereal harmony is created, as magical and as reliable as the first star of evening.

Author's Note

The stories in this collection were written over a long period of time. "Today's Special" is one of the very first pieces of fiction I wrote, and it came about because I was thinking of a friend who had severe problems with depression and who often threatened suicide. Once, sitting at a booth in my favorite diner, I thought, *What if she does kill herself?* I thought of how I would feel, then, sitting there with her gone; I thought of how glimpses of various lives at a diner could have suggested reasons for her not to have done that.

Many of the stories I write deal with the difficulties of marriage. Many touch on the seemingly irreconcilable differences between men and women. But "Ordinary Life: A Love Story" makes the strong point that it can be worth it to work at a relationship.

Marriages are not the only relationships that are looked at in these stories. "What Stays" is about a mother and daughter; "The Matchmaker" deals with the friendship of a young girl and an older woman; "One Time at Christmas, in My Sister's Bathroom" shows a woman coming to an understanding of her difficult father; and "Regrets Only" features a married woman's romantic feelings for her gay best friend.

I want to say a little about the story "Martin's Letter to Nan." In 1996, I published a novel called *The Pull of the Moon.* It's about a fifty-year-old woman named Nan who is dealing with issues brought about by menopause and aging. She takes off suddenly for a trip by herself. She leaves a note for her husband, Martin, saying that she'll be back, but she doesn't know when. *The Pull of the Moon* alternates between letters to Martin and journal entries that Nan makes on her journey. It is a story of self-discovery and self-acceptance, and it seems to have struck a chord in a lot of readers. At virtually every reading I do, when it comes time for questions and comments from the audience, at least one person will mention that novel. Women say they keep it by their bedside. Many say it is their favorite. Some say they read parts of it aloud to their husbands, and one said that it saved her marriage. But the most common question I get is, "What was Martin's response?" "Martin's Letter to Nan" answers that question. Writing the story aroused my wrath at men, but it also made me sympathetic to them. My "significant other" read it with a cigar in his hand, and after he finished reading it, he looked up and said, "This is terrific. You should read this aloud." Perhaps I shall.

I love these stories the way I love my novels, which is rather how I love my children. My children are not perfect, but they are perfect. These stories are not perfect either, but they are the best I could do to portray certain life events, to illuminate certain ways of thinking, to illustrate the way we can get from here to there, to document some interesting insights. More than anything, they are meant to celebrate the extraordinary moments and events that make up ordinary life.

ABOUT THE AUTHOR

ELIZABETH BERG's novels *Open House, The Pull of the Moon, Range of Motion, What We Keep, Never Change,* and *Until the Real Thing Comes Along* were bestsellers. *Durable Goods* and *Joy School* were selected as ALA Best Books of the Year. *Talk Before Sleep* was an ABBY finalist and a *New York Times* bestseller. In 1997, Berg won the NEBA Award in fiction, and in 2000 her novel *Open House* was named an Oprah's Book Club selection. She lives in Chicago.

ABOUT THE TYPE

This book was set in Weiss, a typeface designed by a German artist, Emil Rudolf Weiss (1875–1942). The designs of the roman and italic were completed in 1928 and 1931 respectively. The Weiss types are rich, well balanced, and even in color, and they reflect the subtle skill of a fine calligrapher.